Bella Thrower, a vibrant young author from the picturesque landscapes of Yorkshire, makes her literary debut with *Paris Can't Save Us*. Deeply connected to her roots, Bella draws inspiration from her close-knit family and her love of romance novels. Her love for storytelling began in childhood and she has honed her craft through years of writing and imagination. With her first novella, Bella captures the complexities of human relationships and the resilience of the human spirit. When she is not writing, she enjoys spending time with her family, friends and her young horse.

Bella Thrower

PARIS CAN'T SAVE US

AUSTIN MACAULEY PUBLISHERS®
LONDON • CAMBRIDGE • NEW YORK • SHARJAH

Copyright © Bella Thrower 2024

The right of Bella Thrower to be identified as author of this work has been asserted by the author in accordance with sections 77 and 78 of the Copyright, Designs and Patents Act 1988.

All rights reserved. No part of this publication may be reproduced, stored in a retrieval system, or transmitted in any form or by any means, electronic, mechanical, photocopying, recording, or otherwise, without the prior permission of the publishers.

Any person who commits any unauthorised act in relation to this publication may be liable to criminal prosecution and civil claims for damages.

This is a work of fiction. Names, characters, businesses, places, events, locales, and incidents are either the products of the author's imagination or used in a fictitious manner. Any resemblance to actual persons, living or dead, or actual events is purely coincidental.

A CIP catalogue record for this title is available from the British Library.

ISBN 9781035876808 (Paperback)
ISBN 9781035876815 (ePub e-book)

www.austinmacauley.com

First Published 2024
Austin Macauley Publishers Ltd®
1 Canada Square
Canary Wharf
London
E14 5AA

I would like to take a moment to thank sweet Ella and John, for their extreme generosity. Without them, this novella would merely be an idea stored on a computer file collecting dust.

Claire

Winter is just drawing to a close; the chilled air has begun to thaw, and the sunlight lasts a little longer. I only have five months to go until I successfully achieve my doctorate in medicine. It's been hard, but the thought of coming home to Luke every night gives me the determination to carry on. A two-bedroom semi-detached in Coventry with my fiancé is a far cry from two school kids playing house when my parents were away working, which was almost every weekend.

As a matter of fact, I cannot remember a single weekend since being with Luke when my parents were home. Whether that was because my overbearing father couldn't watch his little girl idealise another man; or whether my mother couldn't face the massiveness of the house which remained since my sister died. The massiveness of the empty rooms with old oak floors highlighted the home's deafening silence and the gaping massiveness which was ever present between the hallway and Pen's bedroom.

Pen's door has not been opened since the tragedy. I mean, death isn't always a tragedy; death is natural, a rite of passage, and sometimes a tragedy. My grandfather dying at ninety-three after a long life raising two children, working until he was sixty and taking a much-deserved retirement to Spain was not a tragedy. It was expected and understood.

However, an eighteen-year-old losing her two-year stint with cancer is a tragedy. It was definitely not understood and not expected. We all expected our brown-eyed, blonde-haired, life-of-the-party Pen to eventually wake up one day and suddenly *be* better. But after losing her eye-catching blonde locks, the fight sort of fell from her eyes. As if the fight was cut away from her just as her hair was taken too. She lost her fight fourteen years ago. My mother lost her reason to fight fourteen years ago.

I'm told I look like Pen. Never that I am *like* Pen. No one was like Pen. Pen was unique. Pen was rain in a period of draught; the cloud shading you from the scorching sun. Pen was the smile on my mother's face, the reason she had me and my brother. I can't help but wonder if she was disappointed that we weren't like Pen. My brother, Joe, and I are more alike, two peas in a pod. From our rich chocolate hair; Pen dyed hers blonde from young—I used to envy Pen—to our olive skin tone. Joe is darker than me, I've always described myself as a poor excuse for olive skin. Light freckles coat my cheeks, giving me a deeper skin tone. We are both shy but not quiet, we don't match Pen's witty sarcasm she seemed to have mastered in the womb. Joe and I much take after our father—small in stature, more of an extra than a main character. In fact, if there was a show based on our family, 'The Higgins Show,' Mother would be the problem solver; Father would be the workaholic with the occasional comment at dinner, Pen would be the main character which the show revolved around, and Joe and I would be waiting staff in the restaurant down the street. I can't help but feel like Pen was the perfect mix of my mother and Joe reflects my father in so many ways, and I am the leftovers, all the unwanted parts formed to create me. It's ironic to be so polar opposite to my sister when our names are practically synonyms, Nelly Claire Higgins sister to Penelope Louise Higgins. I have gone by Claire for fourteen years now.

Hunched shoulders carrying the weight of two, two-hour lectures followed by three hours of studying. Shopping bags pull down my left side as I search through my bags for the door key all while trying to juggle my books. Luke sees the security light flick on, shining attention onto my messy bun and the deep bags under my eyes. Without asking, he wades in from beyond the front door and scoops up all the bags and books I am carrying in one arm. A large, muscular arm accented with a sleeve of tattoos depicting a Roman theme and a faint 'NCH' in the crease of his elbow which he got when we were 17. He's not changed much since then, only updated an already perfect model. Blonde hair, eyes bluer than the Mediterranean, a physique just as pleasantly perfect as the personality which goes along with it. He matches my quiet playfulness with just the right number of comical jokes and affection. It's as if we were created in unison, matched exactly, the mac to my cheese, some would say. I sometimes wake up in the middle of the night and wonder if this is too good to be true.

It is our anniversary on Friday. Luke always has some big surprise planned which tends to embarrass me and results in me falling in love with him even more, all at the same time. He's a good man, great even, never faltered. He follows me upstairs, carrying all of my belongings while playfully tickling my ankles with his other hand as we walk upstairs.

Luke steals a kiss when we reach the landing and whispers, "You get a shower, love. I'm nipping to the shop." I swear his kisses still send shivers down my spine like a fire erupts in my stomach every time his warm lips press against mine.

After the quick and extremely necessary shower after the long day I've had, I walk through our beautiful home to the kitchen. I cannot believe we live here sometimes. Cream walls, an oak staircase highlighted with a glass chandelier and a marble kitchen. Ever since we were young, I'd told Luke that I wanted a marble countertop in my kitchen, the type you see in films before the perfect family sits down to eat together. It radiates unproblematic energy. I proudly stride through our kitchen, gliding my fingers across the marble as I go, and take a seat at the breakfast bar. Spinning on my chair, my eyes widen as they see a bouquet of red roses taking up almost the full counter. Jumping out of my seat like a teenage girl at her first concert, I let out a squeal! I run over to read the card positioned amongst the flowers, almost tripping from excitement, 'you make me breathless.' Those words sliver into my throat, down to my stomach and touch the tips of my toes. Warmth elevates through my body and suddenly I *am* breathless.

I stare intently at the card for several minutes, like the words will melt away if they leave my gaze. All the warmth inside of me is suddenly redirected to my waist, where two hands are gripping me tightly, pulling me so close to them I almost stumble.

"Did you like my card?" My eyes widen, Luke's voice is warm and tender, like a thousand feathers tickling the back of my neck.

I turn with delight to see a broad outline of a man. His hands are still clutching my waist, with each thumb circling my skin where my t-shirt has raised a little. I am so close that I can feel the stubble on his cheeks and the warmth of his breath beating down on me. It sends shockwaves to my heart as it pumps harder and harder. His shaggy, longish hair covers a small scar on his forehead. He watches me as I scan his body with my eyes, he's still awaiting my response. I pull myself up on his shoulders and place my lips on his. I send the electricity he's just given me right back through his body. I sharply inhale as the kiss gets deeper and quicker. I'm taking him in with every breath until I've consumed him. I let out a deep exhale as he lifted me onto the breakfast bar. His hand runs through my hair and down my back, leaving warmth and tingles with every touch. He pulls away; "Happy early anniversary, my love." If my stomach wasn't flipping already, it is now. I bite my lip to hide the smile that he has just plastered across my face. He knows what his words do to me and I don't want to give into his ego any more than I already do.

Luke gives me the once over with his eyes before lifting me from the bar, "I hate to stop what we've just started, but we planned to meet your mother at eight." The bubbles which the last six minutes created inside of me evaporated as quickly as Luke spoke that sentence. I let out a girlish giggle, steal a quick kiss and run upstairs to get ready, shouting as I go, "I love you!"

My mother still lives in our family home with my father, yet *'family home'* is a far cry from the house where I grew up. The décor has not changed since I moved out; a beige carpet still trails the floors throughout accented by a chandelier in the main hallway. As we follow the smell of lasagne to the kitchen, we are greeted by my mother dressed head to toe in pearls—it can never be just a casual Wednesday night dinner. Luke understands the stress which consumes me during these evenings and shoots me a half-smile before taking a seat at the large oak wood twelve-seater table. The table it set for twelve, centrepiece and all, despite only the four of us attending the dinner. My father enters in a two-piece suit and I can see Luke's eyes fall to examine his own outfit; he paired his brown chinos with a white polo shirt and definitely isn't wearing a tie.

Dinner is always tricky; we tend to choose silence over muddling through small talk yet try to avoid anything related to our lost family member, or the speculation over when Luke and I will have a family. Mother chose the latter and brought up how my younger brother Joe's wife was already pregnant. I tossed an eye-roll her way and continued to pick at my lasagne. I try and avoid the family topic altogether; Luke is desperate to start a family, but I would rather wait to establish my career first. Luke squeezes my leg under the table, either to offer support or to make it known that my avoidance did not go unnoticed. After dinner, Luke went into the study with my father to look at a new gadget of his and I accompanied my mother in the kitchen. "Come, dry the pots while I wash and talk to me, is everything okay?"

I felt another eye-roll creep forward as she passed me the soapy plates, "I just don't think pressuring me into having a family is good dinner table etiquette. Luke and I have spoken of having children, but we have agreed to wait until after my career is in full swing and we are financially stable."

She pauses before placing her hands back into the suds, "If that was the case, why didn't you tell us in front of Luke?" I put the dish cloth on the countertop and walk to the refrigerator to collect a bottle of water—this conversation has left me with a bad taste in my mouth. I don't have to come up with an excuse for my mother, she already knows why I kept quiet at the dinner table, "You haven't told him that you aren't ready for a family yet have you?" I hang my head in shame. I have been putting off the thought of having a family for months now; when Luke brings it up, or I sense him about to bring it up, I tend to distract him with something; whether it be a spontaneous trip away or sex, anything usually works. She walked over to me and placed a hand on my shoulder; I assume that she realised she was the only one in the room to offer me some support. We stand there for a few seconds too long before the men return. My mother's hand quickly jolts back to her side as if it would be horrendous to be spotted offering her daughter some comfort. I give Luke the nod to say that I am ready to leave and he fetches our coats. We let ourselves out after sharing goodbyes and we make our way to the car.

It is a quiet twenty-minute drive home other than Luke's few comments about my father's new chainsaw. I nod along with him, hoping that is all the conversation he needs until I can get in the bath and wash the night away. Once we arrive home, I tell Luke I am going to have a well-needed soak. As I wait for the bath to run, I stand naked in our master bathroom. My solitude is invaded by Luke's hands exploring my body. He stands behind me and pulls me towards him, the heat from his body radiates through mine. My eyes close as he kisses my neck intently. Time stops while his lips travel my body until the water begins to ripple over the sides of the tub. My eyes open as my feet feel a splash of the water and I am awoken from my dream. Luke spins me and takes a kiss from my lips, "You can relax by yourself now, you deserve it," and he leaves the bathroom. Once submerged in the soapy water, the words Luke has just spoken repeat in my head '*you deserve it.*' If I deserved it, I would not feel so guilty to be denying Luke of his family. Thirty minutes go by as I tow with myself at the idea of starting a family. I decide to put Luke first and agree to have a baby with him.

I don't even wait to dry myself; I head out of the bathroom in my towel in search of Luke. He is laid on the couch with his eyes closed. Standing there and looking down on the potential future father of my child, a smile sneaks its way to my face. There is a small gap where his feet end and before the couch finishes I squeeze into it so that I can watch him dream. His eyes open, "What were you dreaming about, darling?" He mouths 'You' before his eyes shut again.

I pull myself off the couch and sit beside his face on the floor, "Luke, I think it's time we go to bed." He offers his hand out to me and we both stand before returning to the bedroom. Once in bed, I roll onto my side and brush his golden hair behind his ear. I push my face close to his and whisper, "I think I am finally ready to start a family with you." Before I could lay back, Luke's mouth was already on mine; his smile tried to break through as we kissed. He kisses me deeper and deeper until I am consumed by his lips.

It seems as though I had only just closed my eyes when I am awoken to the smell of pancakes and treacle; I assume that breakfast in bed is Luke's way of thanking me for last night. He kisses me on the forehead as he brings in a tray full of pancakes and a glass of orange juice, "Who knows, we could have a child nine months from today." I smile at him and nod, I don't won't to dishearten him by admitting that it is quite hard to become pregnant while on the contraceptive pill. I had already taken yesterday's before I decided that I want a family; a decision which seemed much less daunting with the security of contraception. Underneath the plate of pancakes, there is a note, 'We are going on a shopping day. Get ready.'

I deliver Luke a smile, which fades from my face as fast as it grew; my eyes float towards the nightstand where my tablets lay. I reach for the drawer and pull out the packet. Swallowing one quickly before any hesitation invades my mind, I decide to shower, hoping to wash away the guilted look from my face before causing any suspicion with Luke. Before I have a chance to get dressed, his hands sliver behind me and to my stomach. He presses his weight against me until I am laid back on the bed. While kissing my neck he whispers, "I don't want to waste any chance we could get." The kisses grow stronger and more passionate as they travel through my body until they find my mouth. As he enters me, I open my eyes to look up at the ceiling. A hurricane of emotions is upon me as I know this act will not result in a child, but Luke is putting everything into trying to create one.

Guilt swarms my face once more and I decide to get another shower. It was around eleven in the morning when we finally left the house. Luke spent the whole day following me around like my puppy. Every shop I looked at, we went inside and every item I touched or glanced at for more than a moment too long, Luke bought me. It was around one before I decided Luke had pampered me enough and we headed for food—another thing that I couldn't pay for.

Two hours later, we returned home. After taking the endless shopping bags to the bedroom, I return to my pyjamas. Luke has a blanket ready for me on the couch and a warm drink. Despite the guilt, I cannot resist a couch nap. Curious as to why Luke hasn't joined me, I sit up and pan the room for him before finding Luke at the sink washing up.

Waking from my slumber, the house is almost unrecognisable. Luke cleaned it head to toe while I slept. A pain in my chest grows as I feel the torment of my actions. Luckily, I have a night shift at the clinic where I intern this evening to act as a distraction. Luke isn't around when I leave, so I decide to make a quick dash out of the front door before my guilt is reaffirmed.

On my way home, I pick up a crate of beers for Luke as it is our anniversary. I set them on the floor of the kitchen, before returning to bed for some much-needed rest. Five hours later, I wake up with Luke still beside me. His hair is wet and drops of water are rolling down his cheeks, outlining his chiselled jaw and down to his collar bone. As he places a kiss on my forehead, a drop rolls onto my face and towards the crease in my lips. "I have booked a meal for us tonight, but it is a surprise." Another guilty smile invades my face.

We arrived at my favourite Italian, 'La Plaza.' It's only a ten-minute drive from our house, you can almost smell the pasta from our bedroom window. I'm so glad he booked here. As we walk towards the door, I take in the beauty of this place. It is a stone building with a large glass window front. This leads directly to the front courtyard, which is covered in a grand white canopy dressed in flowers. La Plaza was truly made for customers to enjoy the summer afternoons with a glass of wine sitting in that courtyard. As we venture inside, the entrance hall is home to a large, breath taking chandelier. When the sun sets, the orange tones are reflected through this masterpiece, creating the most amazing indoor sunset. Amber tones bounce from every wall and corner. Most say the food tastes better at sunset. We arrived in the evening, yet the restaurant was still as special to look at. I spin, taking in the Tudor-style beams above my head, the rustic leather brown chairs, the paintings of Italy sprinkled across the walls. My eyes tighten shut; I stand taking in the aromas of pasta and bread coming from the kitchen. When my eyes open, I see *the* sunset in front of me. Luke is wearing a black shirt, with the top two buttons undone, tucked into his favourite pair of denim jeans. They're my favourite too, they fit him perfectly.

My thoughts are cut short when I feel the buzz of my phone in my jumpsuit pocket. I reach down, and hold my phone, starring at the name for a few seconds before I slide my finger across the screen and hold it up to my ear. My hesitation didn't go unnoticed by Luke, he raised an eyebrow and took a step towards me. He disguises his curiosity by wrapping his arm around my waist, but I can tell he wants to listen to the conversation.

"Claire, I know it's late, but it can't wait until Monday," the voice hurdled through the phone. I wasn't used to hearing John's gritty voice much after 5.30 pm, so for him to call at just gone 7 sparked some interest in me. John is one of the paediatric doctors at the clinic where I intern as part of my degree; if you are on his good side, he will move mountains for you and if you are on his bad side, you best start looking for a new job. Luckily for me, John took me under his wing when I started in his department last August. He has helped me fullish into the practising nearly nurse that I am today, so if John calls me at 7 pm, I will always answer the phone. I shoot Luke an apologetic look as I head outside to continue the conversation with John, half expecting him to ask about my shift yesterday.

To my surprise, John blurts out, "There is an opportunity for a young paediatric nurse to intern over in Paris for a year. They have asked for a handful of candidates which I would like to put forward, but the only name I could think of was yours, Claire." I was expressionless and he continued, "When you arrived in my department, I saw a young woman who was so eager to jump into the career headfirst; you were so passionate about going into medicine to help people like your sister; but you also spoke to me about how much you would love to travel and how much you would love to help people along the way. But the only travelling you have done is around the same clinic day in and day out. This is a perfect opportunity for you, Claire. Before you say anything, I have sent them a detailed portfolio of your work while you have been with us and they are really looking forward to having a conversation with you. I thought you would decline if I had asked you first. Please give it some thought and speak to Luke. Be in my office at 7 am sharp Monday morning. Have a great evening."

Before I had a chance to gather my thoughts and produce a response, the phone call had ended. I steady myself against an ivy-covered piece of wall and decide I should head to the bathroom to compose myself before returning to Luke. As I stare into the mirror while running my hands under the cold water in hopes of awaking myself from the strange dream I have just had, I am taken aback by the countless conversations I have had with Luke daydreaming of a life exploring foreign cities and cultures. Luke and I have always wished to travel, but so far, we have not seen further than the London Eye.

Ten minutes pass before I return to our table, Luke's glass is now empty, yet his curiosity seems to be overflowing. He doesn't greet me with conversation; he is wary of the phone call which has stolen my attention for fifteen minutes too long on our anniversary meal. A smartly dressed waiter breaks the tension to ask for our order. Luke orders a white wine for me and a beer for himself. Before he takes a breath, I jump in, "Make that two drinks each, please." The curiosity bleeds from Luke's eyes and is replaced by worry. We order our food—spaghetti carbonara for me and fish for Luke—and I resight the proposal to Luke word for word. He responds in a similar way to me; his mouth is quiet, yet his face is full of intrigue. "We would move to Paris. For a year? Do you even know any French?" His outlook on the situation is enlightening.

We spent the rest of the evening discussing the prospect of uprooting our lives for a year, dabbling in the very few sentences of French we know, and we even googled apartments to rent over a crème burlier. It was almost midnight once we arrived home and we were quick to clamber into bed after one too many drinks, especially for Luke who was supposed to be the designated driver. He turned to me as I lay there, still with makeup on and one earring in, "Claire, we should go." I kissed him softly as if it was the only way I could communicate with him—we are good at communicating without needing to speak. We had a week's worth of conversations without saying a word before the night was up; it was as if our bodies had synchronised, and even though our minds hadn't come to a decision, our bodies had come to one for us.

What better way to say goodbye to your family and friends than to host a garden party with seemingly too much meat and not enough bread rolls to go around? My mother's garden was full of co-workers, distant relatives and close friends all ready to wish Luke and me a safe journey to Paris. Despite my mother and farther disapproving of the move, they were happy enough to arrange the gathering—my mother feels we are doing our careers an injustice and my father knows who to agree with. If only Pen was here to cheer me on; I like to imagine that she would move with us to Paris if she was here—she was spontaneous like that. We fly in two days, so we have plenty of time to recover from a night of too much drinking and too many goodbyes.

After speaking with the children's hospital in Paris and with an advisor at my university; I will continue my degree part-time and remotely while undertaking a year's internship at the Necker Enfants Malades Hospital. The hospital has sourced a lovely apartment only a fifteen-minute walk away from the hospital with a year's lease and thankfully, Luke works for a marketing firm, so working remotely has been his norm since the COVID-19 lockdown. We have also secured tenants for our home in Coventry, which will help us with the mortgage while we are away. Luke hasn't mentioned the prospect of children, or why we are having trouble falling pregnant since Paris has been in the picture. Paris may be fulfilling enough for him to bench the idea of a family for at least a year.

As the evening draws to a close, my mother hugs me tightly as if she is actually going to miss me. I haven't felt a hug like this from my mother for fourteen years; it is quite bittersweet that I have had to move countries to drag this affection out of her. Countless hugs and handshakes are followed by the rest of the guests as they leave. I can't help but stand in this empty garden, under the twinkling of the fairy lights strung amongst the willow trees and close my eyes to reflect on the evening. My eyes snake around the gazebo in my head as I reply the tonight's events; I see colleagues whom I rarely speak but five sentences to during a normal day; I see distance relatives who continually called Luke 'Liam' for the entire event; I see a group of several friends of Luke and mine who I will miss dearly, but other than that, I will be quite content to leave.

Luke and I arrive home after the twenty-minute taxi ride, leaning our weight onto each other as we make our way upstairs to bed. He looks at me with a drunken haze around him, "This might be the most amazing thing to happen to us."

I nod as tears fall on my face, "I think you're right." More tears fall as I reach for Luke's hand which is resting on the bed. Taking a seat next to him, I look at him for all he is—A perfect fiancé. He bites his bottom lip with his top as if he can see exactly what I am thinking. He looks my body up and down as if I am a book which he cannot put down. He wipes my fallen tears with his thumb before moving towards the spaghetti strap of my A-line red dress, kissing my shoulder where it lays. His kiss is soft and inviting, like is he asking nicely if he can undress me. I feel his teeth take hold of the strap as he pulls it loose over my shoulder. I copy the movements with my hand on the other strap. I gasp and take in a breath as he pushes me back onto the bed. Suddenly, my ankles are at his mouth and he begins to explore my body.

Claire

There is something poetic about arriving at the airport during heavy rain, only to be jetting off to a much warmer location. We hired a minibus to the airport; I thought the goodbyes were already thoroughly exhausted after the leaving party. As Luke settles the payment, I do a last check for passports and boarding passes. We have our lives stuffed into two large suitcases, praying that neither will surpass the 25kg mark. I am taken aback for a moment as we wheel into the long check-in queue; it is hard to compose myself while daydreaming about the life we are leaving behind. The storm in my mind is calmed by Luke's hand on mine, my deep breath is cut off by Luke's lips pressed to mine, "We are doing the right thing."

"Passports and boarding passes please." I hand over our documents to the fresh-faced flight attendant with a smile plastered across her face. "Are you Nelly Claire Higgins?" Pains shoot into my chest. I grimace at the thought of being addressed by Nelly as if it is an insult to Pen to be named so similarly to her. The pains develop into anxiety which stretches across by body and mind. Luke turns quickly to see the results that my own name has caused. A warm hand is placed on the nape of my back and I suddenly feel a release of pressure. Luke nods for me before I receive a curious look from the flight attendant.

After browsing duty-free, we still have an hour to wait until our early morning flight from Birmingham Airport. We decide to muddle over some French phrases while we wait for out gate information over several cocktails and a bacon sandwich each. By the time we are in the queue to board, we have perfected our pronunciation of 'Où sont les toilettes?'

I have always wanted to have someone waiting for me at the airport with my name on a sign. We arrived to just that once we landed in Paris. The taxi ride was lovely and scenic. I spent the whole journey imagining what would come of our lives while being here. Daydreaming off onto a tangent, I imagined Luke as a French baker, who brought the leftover pastries home for me and our children. He would be a great father; his love for me is magical, but I cannot imagine how much love you would feel to be the child of that man. My daydream is suddenly flooded with guilt. Two weeks before we were set to fly, I had the contraceptive implant fitted to prevent the struggle of finding a pharmacist in Paris to prescribe my contraceptive pills if I ran out. Luke is unaware and potentially still hoping for a positive pregnancy test every time we have sex.

I am quickly awoken by the view of our apartment building, which I recognised from the photos online. It is a cream-coloured building in the 14th arrondissement of Paris. Stepping out of the taxi layers of ivy dressed the walls and almost hid the cobbled pathway to the entrance. "Bravar," Luke exclaims as he clutches my hand and spins me in the street. I can see the joy take over his whole face. We thank the driver and head up the cobbled path to investigate our new home. A spiral staircase greets us, and we climb to the third floor. It is smaller than we are used to, and the décor is dissimilar to that of our modern Coventry home, but the view makes this small apartment stretch as far as the eye can see. I dance through the beige-carpeted living room and down the hallway to our bedroom. The walls are painted a lilac colour, with just enough room for a bed and a wardrobe. Before the joy could melt away from Luke, I take his hand in mine to our balcony. I tell him how we can eat our breakfast on this balcony and watch the world go by. It is as if he is so captivated by the view that he doesn't hear me, "Claire, if you look really hard, I think you can see the Eiffel Tower." We stand there for ten minutes in awe of the view and a potential Eiffel Tower in the distance. I am awash with love and appreciation for what an amazing opportunity I have had. I look at Luke and deliver him a kiss on his cheek before heading for a shower.

John sent me a list of lovely A La Carte restaurants to try in Paris; he and his wife travelled to France a few years ago and Luke and I had never been until now. We picked the best-looking Italian on the list after scouring reviews all last week—'La Vie est Belle.'

I pinned my hair back and wore a floor-length crystal blue dress with deep blue heels and Luke complimented me perfectly with a navy-blue shirt and a pair of black suit trousers. We decided to take a leisurely walk towards the restaurant so that we could take in the crisp air and delicate scenery. Vespas and old-timey cars fly by us as we venture through the back streets of our new city. Washing lines hang from apartment windows amongst the strings of streetlights guiding the path to a captivating row of sycamore trees.

Where the trees part, the light from the end of the road sneaks through; 'La Vie est Belle' swings on a rustic sign in the light breeze. Luke squeezes my hand with excitement for our first meal in Paris. The setting sunlight glimmers on a rose bush at the entrance. Amongst the chatter of French from inside, I find comfort in our waitress having a cockney twang. She seats us next to an open window with an enchanting view of a stream in the near distance.

Luke and I share several minutes of silence throughout the dinner as we take in the surroundings and watch various French couples. Between the different drink orders, we find out that our cockney waitress emigrated to Paris 14 years ago with her family. I watch her a lot during the evening, seeing her long brown locks bounce in her ponytail as she flips between French and English, completely unphased. There is something warm about her friendly face, something which reminds me a lot of Pen. I could see her living in France, completely grasping the change of culture and language from the offset. Once the cheque arrived, I asked the lovely stranger her name and complimented her on her likeness to my sister. She was called Nell, after her sister.

I froze. A chill grew in my stomach. I couldn't speak; but even if I could, I wouldn't know what to say. The coincidence is uncanny; I too am named after my sister, who died 14 years ago. I was broken out of my momentary stillness by Luke's rebuttal, "She is called Nelly. What are the chances of that?"

Her eyes grew large with intrigue. "My sister was clearly my parents' favourite, so I was called Nelly after Penelope. She sadly passed away 14 years ago." Our waitress dropped her head with sorrow as if she was all too familiar with the pain that I had been through. She was called away to serve another table, but before we had a chance to leave, she handed Luke a piece of paper with her phone number on it. "If you are stuck for a fellow English friend, or need some advice on the best places to go, please let me know."

Walking hand in hand back to the apartment, Luke and I mulled over the encounter we had just had. I teased the idea that Nell the waitress could be named after my sister. My thoughts spiralled and I suddenly found myself questioning if John, knowing my parents quite well, knew of this waitress and purposely added La Vie est Belle to the list of recommendations for a reason. I found myself distant from Luke and Paris for a few moments and I was back with Pen as a young girl; we were playing hide and seek in the garden; she had her hair in a ponytail and her not yet dyed brown locks were bouncing around just as the waitress' were. I remember being genuinely happy at that moment; a far cry from hiding contraception from your fiancé and moving to Paris to deter the idea of a family even more.

I fell back into reality when a drop of rain landed on my forehead. Suddenly, it was as if the skies opened and buckets of water cascaded down. Luke pulled me close to him as we ran towards the apartment. Laughing hysterically at how sodden we were, we fell inside.

After a shower and cosying up in bed next to Luke, my mind was back to deciphering the hidden message behind our meeting with waitress Nell. I am yet again cut off in thought as Luke turns to me, "Claire, four months ago I asked you about the possibility of starting a family. Before we knew about Paris, you agreed to start a family with me. I know we are now here for a year, but we have not discussed what that means in terms of our future family?" I don't respond and hope that Luke thinks I am asleep. He kisses me on the head and whispers, "We will talk tomorrow." I don't want to talk tomorrow. Luke has always longed for a family, but with my hopefully busy and successful future career, I won't have time to share my love with anyone else but Luke. I thought that Paris would have been enough for him, but clearly, it is not.

We both have a week of annual leave before Luke returns to work and I begin my internship, so waking up at 09.37 is a simple pleasure that I will not take for granted. Luke rolls his body close to mine and lightly brushes my cheek with his thumb. I know he wants to discuss our potential family, but I have bigger things on my mind, such as my potential long-lost sister.

I asked Luke if he wanted to have breakfast at La Vie est Belle again, I noticed a breakfast menu on their outside menu board as we left last night. He steals a kiss from me and leaves the bed to get dressed. I lay there privately for a moment, drowning in thought. When Luke returns to steal a second kiss, I jump up quickly to dodge the looming conversation of family to get ready.

The breeze carries a chill with it, so I lay a denim jacket over a black cotton jumpsuit. Luke walks with his arm tucked over my shoulder; he is pulling me close to him. I love his affection usually, but after last night's confession that he still wants to start a family, I feel withdrawn from him. We are greeted by Nell again at the entrance. Somehow the restaurant's beauty is even more present in full daylight. After taking our order, I confess to Nell that breakfast is not my only reason for coming, "I was wondering if I could ask you more about your family. I have had a strange feeling in my gut that

I was supposed to meet you." Luke shoots me a stern look as if I am overstepping.

"It's okay I don't mind talking about my sister and it is a strange coincidence I must agree. My sister died when I was born, we were twins, but only I made it. My parents named her Penelope, hence the Nell." I breathe in the information that I have just been given; it oozes down my throat and creates a pit in my stomach. I overflow with questions and they all escape at once, "Who are our parents? My Penelope was very much alive and lived until she was eighteen. Is it possible that this is the same Penelope? I need to call my—" Luke grabs my hand and breaks me from my spiral of thoughts. I look up to Nell, who looks dumbfounded. I quickly attempt to apologise.

She shakes her head. "It's okay, it is just a lot to take in at this time in the morning." She excuses herself to greet some customers awaiting a table and I am greeted with a disappointed glare from Luke. I take it that he doesn't think I should've unloaded all of that onto Nell.

"I'm sorry, Luke but that was too much of a similarity, I thought she knew something about Pen." Luke shakes his head and takes a drink of his coffee. Silence swallows our table for the rest of the meal, but it doesn't penetrate my mind. My mind is anything but silent, it is consumed by thoughts of Pen and my parents and Nell the waitress. Before leaving the restaurant, I scan the surrounding tables for Nell, but she is nowhere to be seen. We pay the cheque and leave; Luke marching half a stride ahead of me. I can feel his disappointment from back here.

The front door has only just been unlocked and Luke takes himself back to bed, "I am going to have another hour's rest, please don't tell anyone else they are your long-lost family members before I wake up." He smirks at his comment and leaves. I spend the next hour on my laptop researching Nell the waitress. It is hard as I only know her first name and where she works and every ten minutes, I get a gut-wrenching feeling that I am being delirious, and I should stop. By the time Luke enters the kitchen again, I have found out that her name is Nell Elizabeth Jones. I assumed that she got her middle name from a family member and found an Elizabeth Jones in East London. She is a partner at a law firm along with her husband Micheal Jones.

My laptop was closed before Luke could spy on my research. He leans his head onto my shoulder and kisses it softy. His disapproval must've washed away while he slept. "Come on, Claire, why don't we go on a walk? I've googled that it is about an hour's walk to the Eiffel Tower, but where better to walk than through the city of love." A walk may take my mind off of the suffocating curiosity to know who Nell Jones is, so I place a kiss on his forehead to seal the agreement and head to put my trainers on.

We ponder over our future in Paris and what will happen when we go home. Luke looks hopeful as he drip-feeds in comments about a family and children. I don't want to spoil a beautiful day, so I brush away his thoughts of family by pointing out the little shops and market stalls we pass by. Hanging baskets of flowers are draped from every lamppost which line the cobbled streets leading up to the Eiffel Tower. We make a joke out of pretending we are locals as we walk hand in hand through the small pathways between the apartment buildings, exclaiming 'Bonjour' at every passing couple. Skipping through the aged streets, I look to my left to admire the man who has put his own dreams on hold to follow me to Paris. I hold my gaze for a moment as I wonder whether I should book an appointment to remove my implant, or at least tell him about the deception. Sometimes I tease myself with the idea of becoming a mother. I would joke about how I would be a better mother than the distant one which loss created. Sometimes I wonder whether parenting would be so hard when I would have such a devoted father as Luke.

The hour walk goes by in a heartbeat and before we know it, we are staring at the Eiffel Tower in the distance. It is breathtaking and Luke and I are in awe for several minutes before the sight of the queue extending at least a mile long breaks our concentration. We decide to step out of our local hats for a moment to become tourists. Several hundred photos later at the bottom of the Eiffel Tower, we decide to head towards the queue. Another hour passes before we are near the front and there she is. I see Pen in the distance. I start shouting, "Penelope! Pen, what are you doing here?"

Luke looks at me with the same disappointment from this morning, "Luke, I did see her. She was just there." He does not look impressed. I am certain I saw Pen.

We continue in the queue in silence. Once we are in the lift to go up the Eiffel Tower, Luke brings my hand to his mouth and places his lips against it softly, "I know after meeting that girl yesterday, Pen is on your mind a lot more than usual. It is okay to miss her, Claire, but don't let this take over your life." I catch an escaped tear with my finger and wipe it from my face. Luke is right, it probably wasn't Pen. My own mind is clearly not comfortable at the moment and it is deceiving me. I feel a ball begin to form in my throat; the embarrassment of believing I had seen my dead sister begins to invade me. I squeeze Luke's hand in hopes of calming the sickening feeling which is growing inside of me. "Just look up, Claire." My eyes meet the skyline as the lift doors slide open and I am suddenly calm. Clambering away from the twenty strangers, I pull Luke towards the railing. The sickening feeling has fallen away, just as the ball in my throat has evaporated. I stand there, taking in the mesmerising view of Paris below; I am sure I can see our apartment, but Luke isn't convinced. All my worries have melted away and as I turn to Luke, I can see that his troubles have also been swept away in the wind; we are just Luke and Claire at the top of the Eiffel Tower, enjoying life.

I turn to him, "I want to feel like this every day." Still holding my hand, he puts his arm over my shoulder so that I am close to his chest. Even in the hundreds of people and moderate wind, Luke's aftershave clings to my nostrils like a virus. I am an addict to it; when he occasionally used to work away, I would spray his aftershave on my pillow at night to make sure I could still sense his presence as I fell asleep.

We spend the rest of the afternoon taking pictures and admiring the view from up the Eiffel Tower. We laugh and talk and forget about everything else, it just feels like Luke and me against the world. Two hours later, we make our way down the lift to the base of the Eiffel Tower. I didn't want to leave and return to a complicated world on the ground, but we were both getting hungry. On our way back to the apartment. Luke spots another one of the restaurants from John's list, 'Belles Pâtisseries.' This one was a typical French café as if all French cafés were based on this one. There was a plaque on the door which said, 'est. 1874.' It looked as if most of the furnishings were still the original, if not they mirrored the original. The smell of freshly baked bread filled the café from floor to ceiling.

I was overwhelmed by choice and almost ordered one of everything. We sat with hot chocolates and croissants in one corner of the café next to a window so that we could people-watch while we awaited our takeaway order of macarons. Luke shot me a questionable look when I ordered the macarons. I am not one for deviating from my usual orders, but I saw them and suddenly felt the urge to give them a try. Amongst the dozens of strangers touring the streets in front of the window, a violinist in an old-fashioned three-piece suit strolled by playing a tune—it was like a scene straight out of a musical. Luke pulled his phone out to snap a video of the cheery musician and I laughed and clapped in the background. Just as our takeaway order arrived, I quickly thanked the waiter and ran outside to tip the man a few euros for the performance. It is difficult to comprehend that this is my life for a year; I smile at Luke as he follows me out of the café with my jacket over his shoulder. I skip towards him and take his arm in mine. After playfully skipping with him for a few strides, we begin walking back to the apartment.

Once we arrived back at the apartment, I plated the macarons up and placed them on the kitchen side. While Luke is in the shower, I power up my laptop again. I am awaiting an email from Jones and Partners law firm after sending an enquiry about some legal advice. I tow with the idea of powering off my laptop and continuing the lovely day we have had into the evening, but I cannot seem to shake the feeling that I am just about to uncover something which could change my life. I decide to start looking through Nell's social media while I wait for Luke to return. It looks like she lives the jet-setting lifestyle, yet only returned to London twice in fourteen years. I wonder why she left. She doesn't seem to have any siblings, and she doesn't post much about them. I suddenly remember the phone number which she gave Luke when we first met, he put it in one of the living room drawers in case we ran short of dinner date ideas. I begin rummaging through the drawers in hopes of finding her phone number. Now that she has had some time to digest the information, she might want to talk. I quickly key it into my phone and save her as a contact. When I hear the water stop running in the bathroom, I place it back in the drawer under the TV cabinet.

"You've got an email from a law firm, your phone vibrated, and I saw the name on the screen, is everything okay?"

"It will just be junk mail. I'll have a look and delete it. Don't worry." I think I have suppressed Luke's worry for now, but I need to be more careful.

I part from thought and look up to Luke dressed in only a towel around his waist. "I think that Paris is going to be a good look on you. Shall we stay in tonight?" Luke tries the hide the smile that I have just plastered across his face and delivers me with a nod. I am hoping to get some more research done before I go to work, and it would help if I am at home more with my laptop.

We order burgers and fries from a local restaurant to our apartment and spend the evening in front of the TV laughing and joking together. After eating, Luke takes a hesitant drink of his milkshake before looking at me with his big blue eyes. I can sense the direction in which this conversation is going to head in, but tonight I feel at mercy to him. I want him on this couch, in the kitchen and in the bedroom. I want him to undress me with his hands like he does so well with his eyes. I can see that he is nervous to divulge whatever he has on the tip of his tongue, so I decide to help him. I lean forward and take his tongue with mine. We kiss passionately and he pulls me on top of him. Straddling him, I begin to kiss his neck and quietly moan in his ear. With his hand on my back, he slowly moves it down and underneath me. We are sharing the perfect moment and I am so desperate for him. My mouth moves to his ear, sucking his lobe as he lets out a gasp of breath and moans my name. I jerk up. The hairs on the back of my neck suddenly spring to life. For whatever reason, I didn't recognise the name he called me; I feel an imposter to it like I am a fraud who is hiding behind a stranger's name. He opens his eyes as he notices the change in body language. I instantaneously realise what I know to be right. Looking deep into his eyes I whisper, "I think I want to go by Nelly again."

I go to continue the affection and lean in for a kiss, but he pulls back. "What's happened to Claire?" The lust falls from his eyes and mouth and suddenly the moment is gone. I take my leg from over him and sit beside him again.

"I still like Claire, but Nelly is my name and where better to try a new name than a new country."

I remember when I first asked him to start calling me Claire. We were still so young; I think he put it down to my grieving process and then eventually it stuck. I suppose it may be harder to rewire someone's name in your head after fourteen years. "It might take me a while, love. I will try for you." He places each hand on either side of my cheek and brings my head to his mouth, planting a kiss on my forehead before getting up to dispose of the food wrappers.

Before I have a chance to find another film to watch, Luke has taken it upon himself to go to bed. A sense of dismay approaches me as I hear our bedroom door click shut, Luke has been desperate to make love to me ever since I agreed to start a family with him, but tonight he is okay with leaving me unsatisfied. I decide to seek satisfaction elsewhere and reach for my laptop which has been tightly concealed under the couch. I take the silence as an opportunity to check the email which I received earlier.

Luke

I am awash with emotions. How should one react after being asked to change how they address their fiancé? After fourteen years of 'Claire,' suddenly the woman who lay beside me nightly is known as 'Nelly.' I am beginning to wonder if moving to Paris was just another excuse to delay our family and now that we are here and committed, *Nelly* is having second thoughts.

The loss of Pen has been on her mind since the evening we met the waitress. She is becoming unstable and unlike herself. The beauty of the day captivated me and made me blind to her oddities; but as I lay here waiting for her to come to bed, I could not help but think back on the day. It began with reminiscing of a lovely memory, looking back on walking the streets of Paris with the love of my life. We walked for miles, discussing life and the scenery until she was mistaken by one blonde-haired beauty in the distance. It wasn't until she bought the macarons though that I had suspicions; she claimed they were for her to try, yet on holiday to Italy in 2009 with her family, Claire discovered that she definitely did not like macarons.

Claire and her sister binged on a tray full after all day at the beach—Claire could barely make it through three before

Pen took over the rest of the box. Claire should have remembered I was there and knew she didn't like macarons, yet she has been so blind since we came to Paris—so unlike herself.

It was 2 am before Claire had joined me in bed. I laid there with my eyes shut and back towards the door, half hoping for a gesture of affection as she climbed under the sheets. Within two minutes of opening the bedroom door, she was in bed with her back to me and sound asleep; although she was physically present, her mind was elsewhere. It took me a further forty minutes to fall asleep, I couldn't stop convincing myself that I was laid next to a stranger—even her breathing sounded different than usual.

I awoke first and planted a kiss on the side of Claire's cheek. I didn't want to wake her, so I slivered out of bed and ventured to the kitchen to prepare breakfast. Her laptop was perched on the edge of the countertop, winking at me. I felt as drawn to it as Claire had been the last few days. Despite numerous conversations about how Claire needs to password-protect her devices to prevent a moment like this, she thankfully still has not. An email from Jones and Partners is the most recent—a reply to Claire's query and a call scheduled for tomorrow. Have I imposed too much pressure on Claire to start a family and she thinks that leaving me is the easy way out? My mind is suddenly clouded; a shroud of fog has poisoned my thoughts. My hands fall from the keyboard and my legs go limp. I manage to steady myself on the countertop before easing myself over to the couch to compose myself.

Just as the storm within me begins to settle, Claire wades in and takes a seat beside me. I can tell she senses a problem;

Claire has always been able to read me; she says that my eyes tell her everything there is to know. She places her hand on my lap, the warmth cascades through me. As the heat reaches my chest, I take in a deep breath which is cut short by the heat disappearing. Claire removes her hand and lifts herself off the couch and heads towards the kitchen. As quick as her warmth rippled through me, it evaporated. I feel the loneliness consume me as Claire has left me to tow with my own demons alone. Music begins to play from the kitchen radio, as if Claire is trying to drown out my sorrow which is suddenly filling the apartment.

I have decided to take myself for a run, I cannot be around Claire when the solicitor calls her to discuss the pitfalls of our relationship. I decided to run until my mind felt clear again; consequently, that was fifty-three minutes later. The Eiffel Tower is not a grey blur in the distance anymore, its massiveness is right in front of me. I look at it and do not remember the extraordinary afternoon which Claire and I shared; I only feel intimidation by the structure's enormity. Mentally and physically exhausted, I decide to head back towards the apartment, hoping there are no documents to sign when I return. As clear as my mind became, a mist begins to seep in as I stroll past 'La Vie est Belle.' After five minutes of arguing with the idea, I convince myself that I am heading inside for a coffee.

Nell greats me at the entrance with a look of concern, the half-smile I sent her way seemed to have not calmed her nerves. After being seated, she returns to take my order, "One coffee with milk and hopefully a moment of your time." She was taken aback, yet I could see her curiosity growing, as if she too had been questioning the recent encounter with Claire.

"I don't know what you want me to tell you. I've been looking into it, obsessed over it even. My mother won't talk to me, says how dare I discuss Penelope like that. I'm sorry that it isn't what you want to hear." Nell turns her back and walks my order over to the bar, leaving me with a sense of guilt for her situation. I shake my head, realising the pain we have caused by ever coming in and meeting Nell. While I sit and fight my inner turmoil, the coffee arrives, handed to me by a different waitress. Before she leaves the table, I ask for a pen and a piece of paper. She hands me her pen and a scrap of paper from a notepad in her apron. I scribble on the paper, *I'm sorry.* I fold the paper in half and write *For Nell* with a cartoon smiley face. After quickly finishing my drink, I decide I have outstayed my welcome. Leaving the note on the table, I walk home feeling defeated.

Edging closer to the apartment door, I can hear Claire chatting away to someone. The quiet distant chat develops into a heated discussion as I hear Claire's voice raise, until there is nothing but silence. I assume that the phone call has ended, and it is safe for me to enter. To my surprise, Claire isn't in the bedroom packing her life up to leave me but is sitting on the floor beside the couch with her head between her knees. I stand there bewildered for a moment until Claire's shoulders begin to quiver. I lunge over to be by her side and to console her, hoping the tears are tears of regret. She shivers as I place my arm around her shoulders, her head lifts from her knees and her eyes drift to mine. Her eyes look hollow, whatever conversation she just had has shocked her to the core. I kiss her on the forehead in hopes of instilling some peace back into her. Her eyes drift back to stare at her knees, she points to a small scar on the left one, "I got this when Joe,

Pen and I were playing tag and I fell over and cut my knee on a log."

Her eyes hold the gaze at the permanent reminder of her sister, and I sit in limbo, not sure what to make of this confession. Claire has just spoken to a solicitor about the potential of leaving me and probably how to sell our lovely home and all she can think about is her sister. I fall back from my knees and rest my back against the couch beside Claire. With my eyes closed, I take a few moments to ponder where our relationship took a turn.

Claire

"I asked for an appointment with Elizabeth Jones, I don't want to speak with anyone but her."

An unfriendly voice crackled down the phone, "She is on annual leave at the moment, please could you discuss why you are seeking legal advice and I will be sure to get you to the correct department."

My voice began to raise and quicken, "Well, I don't want to speak to anyone else but her." I crashed my thumb onto the phone screen and ended the phone call. I am flushed with emotion; I feel a war beginning in my mind. Regret pools in my stomach and I fall to my knees. Agony consumes me and all the feelings of losing Pen flood back in. I can feel Luke's presence beside me, but I feel numb to his touch. He tries to console me, but I am not consolable. I have lost Penelope all over again and I ache to my bones.

We are silent for several minutes before Luke picks himself up and the warmth beside me disappears. I hear the apartment door close. He has left me; he saw how ill of mind I am, and he decided to leave me. He probably looked at me and thought that I was in no state to attempt to procreate with, so he left. Since arriving in Paris, our relationship has grown stale.

It is hours before Luke returns home. When he does, he has a gloss to his eyes. I watch him stumble into the apartment and grasp the door handle for stability. I am in the kitchen preparing dinner, yet the beer-stained shirt tells me I will only need to cook for one tonight. Luke is clearly drunk when he falls onto the couch, as he completely disregards my presence. I pour him a glass of water and slam it onto the coffee table beside him, making sure some water splashes over the top to alert his attention. He remains still and unphased.

I eat my dinner alone tonight. Despite having plenty of leftover spaghetti bolognese, I bin the lot. Luke has not lifted a single eyelid since his head greeted the cushion. The only movement is from his chest as it moves up and down—at least I know he is alive. Disappointment radiates from me and consumes the apartment. I stand over him for several minutes, looking at the stranger who is disguised as my fiancé. I leave him resting as a means to prolong the argument we are inevitably going to have when he wakes.

Six hours later, I see his hand lift to his mouth to wipe the drool sliding down his chin. As he opens his eyes to look at me, I notice that they are glassy and squinted as he tries to focus his vision through the mist of judgment. It didn't take him long to pick out my frown from across the living room. He says nothing. As he sits up on the couch, I see the rush of pain surge to his head. His hand follows as he places it on his forehead in hopes of calming the headache. I torment him by allowing the smile to creep onto my face before I go and retrieve some painkillers for him. The silence continues as I refuse to beg for an explanation.

Ten minutes pass and the mist develops into a thick fog. It is hard to distinguish Luke through the vale which dresses the living room. "I'm sorry," he coughs out. His apology bounces off the walls before it flies out of the kitchen window. His apology is ingenuine and has left me with a bad taste in my mouth. I decided to pour myself a glass of merlot to settle to sourness on my tongue. I take my drink at the table, accompanied by the bottle of wine, hoping to avoid the confrontation for longer. As my second glass runs dry, Luke joins me. He looks pale at the sight of my alcohol. "I'm sorry that I left when you were upset. It would've been too hard to comfort you given the circumstances. I want you to come to the decision on your own and not to be influenced by me at all." He is still talking about having children. I thought that Paris would delay him for at least a year, but I think I am going to have to try harder to pretend to want his child.

I lean closer to him, kissing him passionately while attempting to surpass the alcohol smell on his breath. As I bite his bottom lip, he pulls away from me. Shaking his head, he leaves the table. Confusion replaces my judgment as I watch him walk to the bathroom. He wants to have children with me but refuses sex when I try to initiate it. Embarrassment and the feeling of being used blows over me.

After five minutes of being consumed by this suffocating apartment, I decided to take myself on a walk. It is almost midnight and the streets are dark, yet it is not as daunting as walking home on a Friday evening in Coventry. Pulling out my phone, I scroll down the contacts to find Joe's number; I decide that women tend to be a lot safer when they are on the phone with someone. We haven't spoken since I arrived in Paris and I think I could do with some brotherly advice. Joe has been married for three years now and is my go-to for relationship advice. After a few messy ones in university, he has finally found a good one. His wife Lauren is a beautiful ginger-haired princess from Manchester. She has a sharp tongue and isn't afraid of calling Joe out when he does something she doesn't like. She definitely keeps him on his toes. I scroll too far and see Nell's phone number appear on my screen. Before I can think of a reason not to call her, my finger has already pressed on her name. Three dial tones pass, and I end the call. I cringe at myself and quickly delete her from my recent calls in case Luke happens to chance on my phone again.

Joe answers on the first dial, "Hey you. How have you been?" He sounds genuine as if he has really been wondering how I am. Twenty minutes passed and we had only just scratched the surface of my relationship issues; we were too busy talking about home and reminiscing on memories together. I am cut off by the vibrating of my phone on my ear. I pull the phone away and read the name which has appeared at the top of the screen 'Nell.' I watch as it rings, forgetting that Joe is still there talking away to himself. "Joe, I need to go, work is calling. I'll call you later." I answer the call and press the phone tight to my ear, "Hello? I have a missed call from this number, hello." I want to speak, but I cannot. My tongue won't produce the movements that I need to reply, and my mouth won't make any noise. I am expressionless and frozen. The line cuts off as Nell ends the call and suddenly, I get my breath back.

After putting my phone away in my jacket pocket, I realise after walking and talking for twenty minutes that I no longer recognise my surroundings. I tap into my high school French and ask a local for directions back towards my apartment. After attempting to translate the directions back into English, I begin to head back to my apartment. Thirty-something minutes later, I finally recognised the ivy-covered building which I now call home. My mind hadn't focussed on Luke or Pen or Nell during the walk home as being lost in Paris took most of my attention, so staring at the apartment door was the first time that I remembered Luke was in there and hadn't spoken to me since he turned me down earlier.

As the door swings open, I am surprised to see that Luke is still awake. His eyes follow me around the room, but he doesn't make eye contact. His head hangs low as if he is ashamed of himself, or possibly still hungover. I greet him with an empty stare and walk myself to the bedroom. I get ready for bed undisturbed as if Luke is afraid to approach me. I feel like a sitting duck in bed while I await Luke's company. My eyes begin to drop shut after an hour of waiting and I fall asleep without the presence of my fiancé beside me.

I awake with the morning sunrise and I become quickly aware of my solitude in bed. Luke must have slept elsewhere last night, possibly to avoid having to face me. My search for my missing fiancé is cut short as I find him sprawled out on the bathroom floor. His decency remains intact as the shirt he was wearing last night is laid over his naked body like a blanket. I stand in the doorway in awe for a moment, uncertain of what to do in this new and absurd situation that I have found myself in. After venturing to the living room for a real blanket to wrap him in, I came to the conclusion that he carried on the party after I went to bed. Luke was in the next room, treating himself to beer after beer as I lay there forcing myself to stay awake until he came to bed.

By the remanence of six empty beer bottles littered about the living room, I guess that Luke will be out for a while longer. I decide that I don't want to be in his vicinity when he wakes, so I quickly change out of my nightshirt and leave in search of some breakfast.

Luke

The sound of the door slamming wakes me. I feel uncharacteristically hungover. My eyes are heavy, and a thunderous headache beats down on me. I am assuming that the sound of the door was Claire leaving the apartment, hopefully taking all of her anger and judgment with her. After brushing my teeth to remove the taste of alcohol, I go to inspect the level of disarray which I left the living room in last night. I cringe as I drop each beer bottle into a bin bag, holding my breath so that I can't smell last night's antics. When we lived in Coventry, a heavy night out was usually followed by a lazy, quiet day in bed together. We used to eat ice cream together until the local takeaway opened so that we could binge on generous amounts of our comfort food. Today, however, was incredibly different. I am powering through cleaning the apartment while my fiancé is nowhere to be seen. After attempting to vacuum before the noise got too much as it ricocheted through me, I collapsed onto the freshly made bed with my phone.

Only three dial tones echoed back at me until the line was cut off; Claire was avoiding my phone calls. I am unsure whether the sickening feeling in my stomach is from the intense volume of alcohol which I consumed last night, or from the realisation that Claire may be slipping through my fingers. I decide to compose myself and write Claire a letter in hopes that my words will wake her from the nightmare she seems to be trapped in.

After fifty minutes of writing and re-writing, as I try to personify the feelings inside of me, I seal the envelope shut with tape and hide it under the bed; I hear the door swing open. The silent apartment suddenly erupts with noise as Claire begins to sob. Her cries can be heard by me two rooms away and I quickly travel to investigate. Her emerald eyes reflect off of the tears which plague them. They grow large as she watches me enter the room hesitantly. Before I get a chance to console her, her arms are up in defence asking me to back off. "Claire, what's happened? Come here, let me help you."

Her armour does not come down and she begins to edge closer towards the door. I shake my head in a plea for her not to leave. As her arm lowers from in front of her to reach for the door handle, I sweep behind her and wrap my arms around her. She tries to fight me away as if she doesn't want to be calmed, but I refuse to let her leave before I know what's wrong. After five minutes of relentless squirming to break free, she is still.

Nodding her head, she whispers, "Okay, Luke." Hesitant to release her, I kiss her on the forehead first to gauge a reaction. Claire sighs as if the weight of the world is on her shoulders. Loosening my arms around her, I encourage her to walk to the couch with me. I sit, but she stands above me.

"Luke, I haven't been honest with you." I feel the years flash before me as my heart begins to crack. I can feel the darkness setting in as I anticipate her next sentence. She doesn't speak for a moment, as if she is waiting for my response which never arrives until she finally admits her lies, "I agreed to have a child with you, but I cannot have children." Further cracks cut into me as the pain becomes insufferable. I shake my head, begging to stop, but she continues, "I have the implant. I didn't tell you because I thought you would forget about wanting children. I thought I would be enough for you." As her tears dry up, mine begin to flood. I am frozen in thought and struggle to comprehend anything further she says. *I thought I would be enough for you.* Despite owning up to her lies, her deception is still present. She is blaming me as if I have hurt her. She doesn't know the hurt which she has forced onto me. I felt drunk with anger and I suddenly saw a veil of red.

As I gain my consciousness back, I am no longer in the living room. On my knees in bed, I am still thrusting into her. Claire is screaming my name begging me to finish. I slow down my dominating body as I misunderstand how we ended up like this. Claire is face down on the pillow, with my left hand holding her head in place. Her screams are muffled as I begin to penetrate her hard and fast again. After I finish inside of her, I stand up and leave the bedroom, pulling my underwear up as I go. To drown out the sound of her cries, I repeat to myself out loud, "She deserved it. She promised me a child. She said she wanted me. She wanted to have sex. She enjoyed it."

It's been an hour and Claire hasn't left the bedroom yet. I'm not sure whether to check on her, or whether my hugs will still have the same effect on her. After another half an hour, I steadily navigate the apartment until I am in front of the door. It is still open from when I left it; Claire is visible from the doorway, wrapped in a tight ball at the top of the bed. She is naked and shaking. I shrink to the floor as I come to terms with what I have just done. With my head between my knees, I too begin to shake. Unsure whether I feel regret, disgust or disrespect the greatest, the splitting headache from this morning makes a reappearance. Sobbing in unison, Claire and I are suddenly on the same page about something—about how disgusting my actions were. As my eyes close between every falling tear, flashbacks of the heinous act engulf my mind. I can hear her screaming for breath; for me to stop, but I don't. I can see everything that I've done, but as if I was on autopilot and something else was in control of my body.

A lifetime passes before I pluck up the confidence to utter any form of sentence. After all that time thinking, the only thing which I can verbalise is, "I can't believe this." I'm not sure what I can't believe exactly; whether that may be how my life has altered so drastically in the last forty-eight hours; or how easy it was for me to allow myself to do that to Claire.

Claire didn't respond. I imagine that she did in her head, though.

Claire

He didn't.

No, wait, he did.

Luke has just forced himself inside of me and raped me.

How is that sentence now a part of my repertoire? That sentence should not exist, and yet it feels more realistic than the last few days of my life. I cannot move. My mind is as frozen as my body. I feel infant-like and vulnerable. I quiver with fear as he stands and watches me. I don't need to look at him; I can sense his presence. The air has become heavy and the hairs on my arms are standing on their end. My head starts to feel fuzzy and my breathing quickens. Hyperventilating begins. Nothing will calm me.

I can't believe this. I also can't believe how a person can complete such a debilitating and humiliating act on another person. I begin to rock back and forth praying that this will sooth me as it did as a child. My moment of respite was severed by a cold, iced hand hovering over my thigh. I felt my warmth flee as he attempted to salvage whatever relationship we had left. Unfortunately, I don't have the energy to move from his clutch, so I sleep.

I attempted to sleep off the pain in hopes that this was a bad dream. Yet when I awake, I still feel the emptiness inside of me. I feel a breeze whistle between my naked legs, and I am reminded of what happened between them. Lifting my heavy mind from the bed sheets, I seem to be alone with my thoughts. Luke must have left the apartment to escape his guilt. I understand how wrong rape is and I refuse to let myself show a blind eye to Luke's actions, but does he deserve prison? Luke has a great job and massive potential in front of him; I would hate to tarnish him with a criminal record. My head begins pulsating as I battle with my thoughts and a migraine begins. I collapse back onto the pillow and sleep again. I feel safer in my dreams than in the real world right now and I would rather imagine myself happy than deal with my pain.

I am woken by the sound of Luke's voice in the kitchen. What was once a wholesome reminder of who I am in love with, is now a scary flashback to the worst night of my life. Rolling over in bed, still completely naked and un-showered since the *incident,* I check the time on my phone to see that I have been asleep for nine hours, yet my exhaustion hasn't subsided.

After dragging myself out of bed, I finally manage to pull on a loose-fitting tracksuit—I can't bear the thought of something being so tight to my skin. Stumbling into the hallway, he is there. Sitting on the floor with his back leaning against the wall, he is there. As if he is a puma stalking his prey, waiting for me to leave the bedroom so that he can pounce. His mouth grew wide as he traced my body with his eyes; I didn't even want to imagine the dirty intrusive thoughts which he had right now. My mind is blank until his eyes reach mine and suddenly, I have clarity, "I don't think we should see each other anymore, Luke." The blue pigment drained from his eyes and as his world collapsed before him, his head hung low.

Several moments of silence pass and Luke deteriorates into the floor. His forehead pressed against the wooden slats; I see his shoulders begin to shake. His voice is mute as if he knows that no amount of trying will convince me to stay with him. I am ready to walk away from this relationship.

Luke

It has been a hard month. My week's leave was over, and I had to go back to work, all while trying to navigate a foreign country *alone*. I am determined to stay in Paris and to fight for the relationship which I so incredibly destroyed. When I looked in the mirror this morning, I didn't recognise myself. My hair was a little more shaggy than usual and my eyes were dull and acutely accented by dark circles underneath. My clothes hung off me and instead of complimenting me, they slandered me. My fingernails were bitten back to a stub from my constant anxiety and worry. It is as if overnight I had become a shell of my former self.

Scuffing the pavement as I shuffle along the high street, a pigeon decides that I am the ideal candidate for its new toilet. My hair hasn't been cut or brushed in weeks, giving it a 'bird's nest' sort of look, which is quite fitting. I swiftly pick my feet up and head towards the nearest café in search of a bathroom. Scrubbing my most recent present out of my hair, I suddenly come to the realisation that maybe I have hit rock bottom; 'café au lait,' I order at the counter, hoping that this coffee fills the vast hole inside of me which my relentless self-pity has created. A beautiful blonde French lady served me my lonely order along with a cheeky smile. Although a harmless gesture, all I could think about was how this friendly stranger was not *my* Claire.

I allowed my mind to spiral while sipping my cup of respite. I thought about how Claire is not *my* Claire anymore, and may never be *my* Claire again. If that is the case, what if this is me now? What if I am the sort of person that harms women like this? Maybe I order another coffee and flirt with this enticing stranger until we end up on a date. That restaurant might close early before we are ready to part, so we take the party back to my apartment. What if we have a few too many drinks and end up doing something that we both will regret in the morning? And what if I get too carried away and refuse to stop when I hear her muffled screams? What if I like that she is struggling, and it makes me want her more that she no longer wants me? What if this is me?

"Would you like a refill, sir?" I shake my head as I jump up from the booth. Hastily walking to the door as I find my coat sleeve, I leave the café, and if that girl is lucky, I won't go back. An hour passes and the sun is setting on the city before me, yet I am still running circles around my own thoughts over my newfound identity. I cringe at every attractive woman I pass as my mind flickers to the things that I could do to her and that I did to Claire. I stroll into the bar which I have commandeered as my second home since the start of this ordeal. The bar man is English, so I feel a little closer to home with every drink that I order. I decided last Tuesday that I will drink here nightly until what happened is erased from my memory, or I become an alcoholic— whichever comes first.

It is now Sunday and I can still smell the perfume that Claire was wearing. In fact, I can still feel the anger that I felt when Claire revealed her lies to me. I usually start the evening feeling sad and sorrow for myself and by nine o'clock, the anger surfaces and I forgive myself for what I did. I am in a constant state of wanting to chase that feeling of forgiveness, and as it usually starts at beer number five; here is my happy place.

I have taken up a habit of people-watching to lengthen the time between mouthfuls of beer. On average, three couples argue in here a night and I can't help but wonder if any of those couples are in a position like Claire and me. There is one man who drinks alone like me every night. He arrives at five o'clock and has four gin and tonics and leaves at seven o'clock. He doesn't utter a word to anyone—even the bar man knows his routine so there is no need for any conversation. He rarely makes eye contact with anyone but the peanut dish in front of him. I spend most nights between five and seven conjuring up a story for this man, one which hopefully makes my own look harmless. I have come to the conclusion that the only way this well-dressed, suited and booted businessman would come to a dark and dingy bar like this is because he is having an affair. The freshly shaven, well-toned man would only want the escape of a back-alley bar to serve as a quick pit stop before returning to his wife and children. The dismal atmosphere and sticky floors will make him feel better about his life, like he is actually doing something right and at least he doesn't work here. His wife must be a well-to-do lady and wouldn't be caught dead in a scene like this, so it acts as a safe haven for him to unwind without the fear of being caught out.

I stumble out at ten o'clock and head to my apartment. I had to find something quick after Claire and I separated and a one-bedroom apartment in the back streets of the outer city was the best that I could do. There are few windows and the windows that I have are murky and the latches are broken or rusted. I couldn't afford to furnish the apartment, so I have had to make do with what was left in it. I have all the basics, like a bed and a working shower, but just a rugged brown armchair in the living room and no TV. There are no carpets or cushions and just a clothes rail in place of a wardrobe. I am taken back to my university life days when I lived on pot noodles and beer—which is quite similar to my current situation. Most nights I don't make it to my bedroom, I am swallowed by sleep once my back hits the armchair; an uncomfortable sleep is the least that I deserve. The burgundy walls which blanket the entire space help burry the little light which enters through the windows, offering me the unique opportunity to be able to sleep in any of the rooms.

Claire

It's strange how I feel so detached from the reflection staring back at me. Last night I decided to dye my hair blonde (*I* being an overpriced French stylist). As impulsive as it was, I was due a change. The piercingly bright strands which twinkle back at me in the mirror are screaming to be shown off to the world. I brush through my new blonde bob with my fingers as I head towards the apartment door.

In a white knitted jumper, paired with a red checked skirt, black tights and leather knee boots, I head out for a coffee. Another English girl is in the same intern program as me and I asked her to meet for a drink; we are both desperate for friends in this new and lonely city. Emily has crisp red hair and has also just come out of a long-term relationship. Her ginger bangs and rosy cheeks emulate her timid personality. We are the same age, yet I feel like I have taken her under my wing. Skipping down the cobbled streets, the flowers are suddenly blooming brighter than they have all month; the sky seems to have cleared from the murky clouds which plagued them, and the air even smells sharper than it did. Emily lives a few blocks away from me, so we decided to meet in the middle. Rows of market stalls and shops carrousel past my eyes as I venture towards Emily, using all of my will power to not stop to ponder at the colourful scarves.

"Excusez-moi," in a half-decent French accent is suddenly spluttered in my face,

"You must be English," he smirks. He clutches his hand onto my shoulders as he steadies himself on his feet; however, it is me who needs steadying after that smirk radiates through me. As the smirk morphs into a calm, closed-mouth smile, the mysterious stranger combs a piece of his dark-mopped hair behind his ear. His fingers then slide down his sharp jaw, until they fall back down to his side. As I trace the stubble on his face with my eyes, my mouth gapes open for a moment too long. The handsome stranger holds his royal blue eyes on me as he asks for my name. Blood suddenly rushes to my cheeks and I can feel myself diminishing as he holds his stare. I stumble over my words as I try to remember what he asked me in the heat of our interaction.

"Hi, I'm Nelly and yep, English." There is that smirk again. He pulled his tan trench coat tight around his body, as if he suddenly got a chill, nodded and began to turn around.

"Nice to meet you, Nelly, hopefully, it won't be the last time."

As the dashing stranger walked his six-foot body away from me, I pondered over our encounter, *hopefully, it won't be the last time.* I am a hopeless romantic, but even I know that the possibility of us meeting ever again is slim to none. It is quite sexy and mysterious how he has left our lives up to chance. I am quickly jolted out of my own imagination by a text from Emily ushering me to hurry up. Lost in my own thoughts as they teased at the potential of this new attraction, I slumped towards the coffee shop, extending the walk a little more with each step. I hoped that the longer I was outside, the more chance the mysterious stranger had of finding me again.

Emily's sweet and innocent face is accompanied by a pink cardigan and a simple black jumpsuit. Her pressed lips grow into a smile as her eyes catch me walking through the coffee shop door, "Bonjour," she exclaims playfully. I respond with a small burst of light laughter as I take a seat across from her. After just ten minutes into our coffee date, Emily notices that my attention is elsewhere, and I have to fess up about the mysterious gentleman. We spend the rest of the afternoon creating made-up scenarios where this god-like stranger manages to fall back into my life. It has been fun to dance around the idea of a new love interest, rather than assuming that I should write off love completely after my previous horrible experience. I haven't told Emily the full script of the horror film that is mine and Luke's relationship, but she knows the basic plot and the ending, so she is all for me jumping back on the dating horse.

Hours seem to pass in the blink of an eye and Emily is waving at me from across the street. Suddenly I am hopeful for the chance of a future without Luke. The positivity elevates me above the clouds as I glide back to my apartment. I remain on this high for what seems like months, and all of a sudden, Christmas surprises me. For the past two months, my life has been on auto-pilot while my head stands firm in the clouds. I haven't decorated for Christmas and I haven't even started looking at presents for my family—Joe texted me last week a picture of his plane ticket to come and visit over Christmas, so it would be rude not to get him a little something. With just less than a week before Joe flies in, I pull on a tatted knitted sweater-dress and thick black tights before sliding on some over-slouchy boots and heading to the nearest high street. Skating across the pavement as if it were ice, I lunge towards a quirky gift store that catches my eye.

Focussed a little too much on the vintage records in the window, I crash into the human barricade in front of me. "Paddon, Paddon," I exclaim with my hands over my face to shield me from any incoming embarrassment. Between the fold of my fingers over my eyes, I see two rows of glistening teeth begging for a response. It is not the teeth which I recognise, it is the lips. Those lips would be hard to forget as I have imagined them pressed up against mine vividly for months now. I explored his angelically smooth jaw with my eyes as I travelled up his freckles to the two pools of sea ready to swallow me. My hand slowly lowered from my face and my mouth began to gape open. His eyes narrow on mine.

"It's Nelly, right? You're the English girl." I watch unresponsive for a moment as his eyes wander my body for confirmation. The only expression that I manage to form is a slight nod of my head. His grin grows into a large smirk as if he anticipated this meeting, "Please talk to me, it's nice to hear from a friendly English face." My pressed lips crease as I try to hold back the inevitable smile that he is about to put on my face and a flirtatious laugh escapes in the process.

After serval seconds of regaining my composure, I manage to muddle out, "I never got your name when we first met." A mischievous look plastered itself across his face while he leant towards me. The strand of hair which was resting on his eyebrow brushed my cheek and I suddenly became highly aware of our closeness. I held my breath and pressed my fingernails into my palms, resisting the lust which is screaming from inside of me. "I'll tell you my name next time." His confidence has me infatuated. As he pulls his head away from my ear, he swipes the corner of his bottom lip again my cheek and I melt.

Trying to laugh off his luring demeanour, I joke with him, "That's if you are lucky enough to see me again."

His confident smirk moulds into a soft and inviting smile as he contemplates his response, "What about in five minutes at the bar across the street?" While I am still digesting his quite forward question, his muscular physique is already striding towards the bar. My feet make a hasty decision to follow the intriguing stranger.

Not sure if I was lost in thought while tailing my new curious companion, but he seemed to have arrived with enough time to order a bottle of wine and find a lantern-lit table close to the outdoor heaters. There is a seat across from him and a stool placed next to him; strings of fairy lights illuminate the outdoor seating and, what I can only assume is a symphony from a French violinist, spills out of the bar's windows. I don't believe that I have ever been attracted to someone's hands before, but as he gestured for me to sit next to him on the stool, I found an odd amount of arousal in those four fingers and thumb of his. Everything feels heightened. As my knee caught his knee as I took my seat, someone might as well have set me on fire. My skin erupts into flames with his every passing sweep of my skin. As I try to concentrate on controlling my intense need for him, he catches me off guard, "It's Matthew."

M-A-T-T-H-E-W. I have never met such an attractive Matthew. I whisper it back to him as if I am sucking on every single syllable as it spills out of my mouth and dances towards his ears.

As the evening develops, I learn that Matthew is in a gap year after finishing a law degree. He grew up in London with his mum and brother in a small apartment. He didn't speak much about his dad, but in all honesty, I lost track after the fifth or sixth sentence. His eyes engulfed me. I was swallowed by them. Frankly, he could have given me a run-down of his weekly food shop and I still would have been content to gape over him all evening. Five hours, three bottles and a hell load of complimentary peanuts had passed, and Matthew decided it was time to walk me home. Understandably, I was quite merry, yet Matthew didn't waver from his dominating exterior. With each step closer to my apartment, the lust grew more intense. I asked him to take me upstairs, which he kindly obliged. My apartment was untidy and cluttered, but he seemed to confidently navigate himself to my bedroom.

With my hand in his, Matthew made quite the tour guide of the flat. He was gentle and tentative as he looked at me intimately. As he sat on my bed, I took a seat close to him knowing that our legs would accidentally touch, and I would feel the warmth hit me again. One of those attractive hands of his appeared on my cheek and brushed over my lip with his thumb. He passed me a slight nod which was followed by a gentle kiss on the forehead. A kiss which penetrated all layers of my skin as it travelled from my head to my toes. I took a generous amount of time to replay Matthew's act of kindness in my head and once I dropped back into reality, Matthew had gone.

Luke

I have been contemplating for a few days whether I should reach out to Claire or not—it is Christmas time after all. Today I have decided that I will go over to her apartment and drop off some flowers for her. We haven't seen or spoken to each other in nearly five months now. It has been a long five months of torture, drinking too much and a lot of anger. I finally feel stable enough to confront Claire regarding my actions and the night that ended it all. As I look in the mirror, a smile reflects back at me for the first time in a while. My fresh haircut and shave reveal the familiar face that I once knew—the face that Claire fell in love with. I've decided to dress casually, in a pair of dark blue denim jeans and a flannel shirt. I've unbuttoned the top three buttons, so Claire doesn't think I'm dressed too formally for the occasion. Sliding on my black high-top Converse, my shaking hands attempt to open my front door.

Walking down the streets with the map on my phone as guidance, I am struggling to calm my nerves. What should be a thirty-minute walk, has turned into the longest thirty minutes of my life. The cold winter air feels like ice on my cheeks. My hands are exposed to the freezing wind as I hold the flowers out in front of me shielding them from being crushed by my shaking body. It has only just turned one in the afternoon, yet the dull sky resembles that of an early winter's evening. As I trudge along the slippery cobbled path, I don't see the same vibrant atmosphere that I once loved about Paris. The streets are void of music and life, really personifying how void of life I currently feel. Claire's apartment is looming, I can see the ivy-soaked walls in the distance. Nostalgia cascades over me and takes my breath; the apartment building in which Claire and I found a home, is suddenly a stranger to me. I take a few moments to collect my thoughts before I pluck up enough courage to head towards the door. My heart is pounding out of my chest. My knees feel weak and they can barely pick my feet up off the floor with each step. My mind seems to blank and suddenly my eyes open and I am at what was *our* front door. My hands struggle to form a fist as I attempt to knock.

One small tap is all that I can muster up. Claire doesn't answer. I fall back into the wall behind me and my body slides down it as I melt into a ball of my own self-pity. As my head is between my knees, I feel weak and my legs slide across the floor until they are straight. I feel unconnected from my body. I feel like I am dreaming, and I am watching our relationship back in my head as if it were a film. I remain quite content as I indulge in the replay of events until I watch *that* night back. I am watching what *I* did to Claire. My body begins to shake uncontrollably for several minutes—until it stops.

A warmth swarms my body and mind and I am suddenly at peace. When I force my head to look up at my saviour, I don't immediately recognise the face staring back at me. Two blonde ponytails hang low beside a familiar face. I am frozen. Claire is different, this isn't *my* Claire. As she kneels beside me with her left hand on my calf, I realise that she has changed—evolved even. Her touch wasn't even recognisable. She looks happy. As I am silently studying the stranger in front of me, she whispers, "What are you doing here, Luke?" My eyes roll to the bunch of roses laid at my side. "I don't need flowers, Luke. You need to leave."

As she tries to remove her hand from my leg, I lunge forward and hold it in mine, "Claire, please just speak to me." Her expression remains unchanged. Her face doesn't light up like it used to when we touched. I loosen my grip and she stands above me. She turns and her blonde ponytails blow to behind her shoulders. I watch the back of her as she walks into the apartment.

As the door is about to close, she raises her voice and prominently states, "I go by Nelly now." The door slams shut and my heart aches. The sound of my heart shattering feels amplified, as if Claire will be able to hear it through the door she has just put between us. I sit in silence, unable to move for several minutes too long before I attempt to drag myself up. I decide to leave the roses at her doorstep, acting as a reminder of me when she next leaves her apartment.

As my slumped shoulders carry my heavy head away from her door, tears begin to travel down my cheeks. I am suddenly flooded with emotion and the regret of losing Claire infects me. The only method I have discovered these past few months which calms my nerves, is to drown them. A forty-minute self-wallowing walk later, and I arrive at my second favourite place in Paris—the first is right at the side of Claire.

After four, maybe five drinks, I begin scrolling through my phone. Years of memories are hitting me from every angle as my finger slides down the screen panning through the several holidays and countless Christmas' together. Another three drinks pass and I decide that I am not going to go lightly. I flip to the contacts list on my phone and scroll down to her name frantically. Staring at the screen as the dial tones ring on the loudspeaker, I contemplate hanging up when a timid voice appears through the speakers, "Hello, who is this?" Taken aback in my bar stool as I realise, she has deleted my number, I am unsure how to respond. My palms begin to sweat as she repeats, "Who is this? This is Nelly, do you have the right number?" *Nelly*, who is *Nelly?*

My breathing quickens and I am suddenly aware that she can probably hear how tense I am through the phone. I take her off speaker and press her to my ear as I take the last swig of my beer and leave the bar. While sweat coats my forehead and the palms of my hand, I whisper into my phone, "Hi, it's Luke—please don't hang up, Nelly." The line is silent for a few moments and then it goes dead. She hung up on me. With my self-esteem dragging on the floor behind me, I head back to my apartment.

I am only a few minutes away from my lonely room when my phone alerts me that I have a text. Still in my drunken pit of sorrow, I pull my phone from the tattered pair of jeans which seem to be hanging off of me. My eyes suddenly widen and with this one text, I sober up completely:

Hi Luke, it's Nelly. Well, it's Claire to you, but I go by Nelly now. You really caught me off guard today, I didn't expect to see you. A lot has changed with me since we saw each other last and I don't feel like the same person anymore. I am not ready to forgive you for what happened, I don't know if I will ever forgive you, to be honest. I will agree to meet you for coffee tomorrow if you are free. I am not promising anything, but we can just talk. I don't know how I will feel when I see you, so if it gets too much, I think I will have to leave. Meet me at the coffee shop across the road from my apartment tomorrow at one if you can.

It is nearly freezing tonight, but I am warmer than I have been for months. I skip back to my apartment with a smile plastered across my face. Running to my bedroom, I kick off my shoes and take my t-shirt off as I go; I have never been more excited to go to sleep before. In my plain and deary bedroom, my imagination runs wild and paints my mind full of hope for tomorrow.

Claire

As I sit here, nestled in the corner of a quiet coffee shop with a hot chocolate, I contemplate what I am doing waiting for the man who raped me. I am huddled in my coat and scarf swinging my legs against the brown leather booth I chose as sanctuary for this meeting, ready to jump up and leave if I feel too uncomfortable when I am faced with Luke's chiselled jaw and ocean eyes. I deliberately chose this tattered-looking café in hopes that there would be little to no prying eyes when I inevitably burst into tears.

    The bell rattles as the door opens and my chest begins to pound. The ringing in my ears suffocates the sound of my thunderous heartbeat. As my stare is glued to the black and white checkerboard style tiled floor, a pair of black shabby Converse slide into view. My palms remain sturdy on my knees, gripping my legs to steady the tremor. My beaded eyes follow his feet as they slide into the booth and sit across from me. Swallowing the frog in my throat, I raise my head slowly. Taking in his smart brown tapered trousers and his well-worn navy-blue sweater, my eyes consume him. I feel like I am looking through a highly focussed camera lens and all the surroundings are blurred. I can only see Luke. Despite everything, I can still only see Luke.

"Hello, you look stunning," he dishes me half a smirk, subtly encouraging a response from me. I raise my head completely now, allowing that half a smirk to devour me. He looks different now, yet still the same. He has more stubble dusting his chin now, yet his lips still frame his face perfectly. His eyes are accented with dark circles now, yet I could still get lost in them. "What are you thinking about, Nelly?" Hearing my name whistle through his teeth causes the hairs on the back of my neck to stand to attention. Luke is so used to seeing me as *Claire*, yet he seems to have finally accepted me for who I am—He sees me as *Nelly*.

Three cups later, we are still frozen to the chairs we sit on; we become lost in getting reacquainted with each other. My cheeks ache from smiling and giggling at Luke's witty comments and it's as if we haven't lost any time being apart. "Where are you staying now?"

His head falls a little, "It's nothing special, I took the first place I could find." Suddenly, something comes over me.

My stomach begins to turn with excitement and anticipation. I know that what I am about to say, I will probably regret tomorrow. I lean forward so that our mouths are near touching and I whisper to Luke, "I would love to see it." I can feel his breath quicken as it blows on my mouth and his eyes widen with his ever-present nerves. My smile drops to a straight face and my eyebrows narrow in, "Don't expect anything, Luke." He shakes his head as if he is offended by my assumption and stands up to pay the cheque at the counter. The few minutes that he is away from the table, I collect my thoughts. Here I am, with the man that I loved an incredible amount, the man who destroyed the trust I had for him and destroyed the person that I used to be. Yet still, in this moment, none of that seems to matter.

"Are you ready?" I take in a deep inhale, reassuring myself that I am okay and stand to follow Luke to the door. Fifteen minutes into the walk to Luke's apartment, he has taken me down almost every side street and turn possible. I cannot help but feel he is stretching this journey as much as he can. We have been quiet while we walk, only sharing the odd snippet of conversation. As our hands swing beside one another and every once in a while, glide into each other, I feel a spark of connection which I can only assume is definitely not one-sided. Lost in thought as we skip through the Parisian streets, I miss the grey six-storey block of flats until I am stood directly underneath. I begin to scan the building's small windows and unappealing skin for a moment, until Luke walks ahead of me and to the entrance. My head jolts between the building's rustic exterior and the back of Luke's head several times; I cannot believe this is where he lives, this is where I made him live because I made him leave.

Following him up four flights of stairs into a dark hallway, he escorts me into his dark apartment. The place is bare and cold, almost no furniture and Luke has not put his mark on the place at all. I am awash with emotion and begin to cry. Luke rushes over to me concerned, "What is wrong? Is this too much? Do you need to leave?" I shake my head but cannot speak. I feel all too responsible for Luke's living position. This amazing man has been living in this depressing atmosphere because of *me.*

Luke's comforting arm around my shoulder guides me to his beaten-up armchair. He kneels on the floor at my feet and rests his hand on my knees, offering me a comforting stroke by his thumbs. We sit like this for a few minutes, the silence between us broken by my sniffling cries. Wiping my nose, I splutter, "I'm sorry that you're living like this, Luke. I don't even know what to say to you, I am so conflicted. I wish Pen was here—she would know exactly what to say." My head falls into my hands and the tears continue to flood from my eyes. The flood gates abruptly close and my body begins to tingle when Luke's lips are pressed against my forehead. Surprisingly, I am not repulsed by his touch as I imagined I would be, rather his tender kiss is carried through my body, warming me from the inside out. The hatred and anger which I have carefully cultivated throughout these months for Luke now feels trivial.

I stand, pushing Luke away from me as I leave the chair. Brushing my hands through my hair, I attempt to collect my thoughts. I stumble towards the door, my mind fogged with confusion and reach for the door handle. With a moment of hesitation, I turn the handle, looking back at Luke and with a half smirk I splutter with a tearful voice, "I'm sorry, it has been lovely, but I need to go." Luke throws me an understanding nod and I leave his apartment.

Almost instantly, tears begin to fall again. I have never felt so conflicted. Stumbling through the streets of Paris, struggling to read the maps on my phone through the tears, I decide to wallow in self-pity over a coffee and slice of chocolate cake in the nearest bakery. Sniffling at the counter, a familiar English voice concerningly asks if I am okay. Embarrassment washes over me and replaces my misery. I didn't think this man could become more attractive but dressed head to toe in chef's whites really accentuates that smile. I wipe away the tears with the sleeve of my tattered cardigan before returning the cheeky grin. I nod at him for reassurance and place my order before taking a seat with the perfect view of the alluring baker.

Despite having two waitresses working, Matthew delivered my order personally, "Here you go. A beautiful slice of cake for a beautiful lady. Cheer up please, a smile looks better on you." Trying to resist the smile, which is eagerly creeping onto my face, I giggle into my hands. "My shift ends in half an hour. Wait for me and you can tell me all about who has upset you then." I am not usually the sort to take up a date from a seductive stranger, but after the afternoon that I have had, I am compelled to accept his offer. I spend the next thirty minutes watching him work between scrolling on my phone and taking sips of my coffee. Every now and then I am greeted with a wink or a smile, and every time I almost fall off of my chair. Just as he waves to me to announce the end of his shift, my phone screen illuminates with a text, *Hi Nelly, I'm sorry about earlier, I can't imagine how difficult things are for you. I will make this up to you and I will get you back.* I can sense my pulse quickening and decide instantly that responding to that text will only encourage more conversation and I am not ready for Matthew to catch Luke's name on my phone and result in me having to explain the whole situation to Matthew, that is a can of worms I am not ready to open.

"You ready? I've got us a few things and we're going to go have a picnic." Tapping the wicker basket at his side, he offers me his hand. I almost jump at the chance to hold his hand and we leave the bakery. It is dark out and the air has a chill to it, causing me to shiver as soon as we step outside. Immediately, Matthew reaches into the basket and pulls out a grey woollen blanket and wraps it around my shoulders.

Suddenly, there is no need for the blanket as I feel all warm inside. We walk down some unfamiliar streets until he announces, "We're here!" and I stand in revelation. The site of our picnic is a courtyard on the peak of a small hill, creating the perfect viewing platform for the Eiffel Tower and the surrounding city. Strings of lights float around the perimeter of the area, guiding the way to various picnic tables and apple trees. Despite the abundance of tables, Matthew pulls another blanket from the basket and places it on the ground at the very edge of the courtyard, assumingly so that we have the best view.

Matthew changed before he left work into a pair of black casual joggers and a grey hoodie. It is quite intimidating how a man can dress so casually, yet still remain incredibly attractive. We didn't say much for the first several minutes, I guess we were both taking in the star-lit city and listening to the occasional rustling and chirping from the trees around us. He cuts the silence by revealing the contents of the basket, pulling out a bottle of wine and two glasses, two slices of the chocolate cake which I ate earlier and six different sandwiches all with different toppings. "I didn't know which one you would prefer, so I made a few."

I can't help but laugh at the trouble he has gone to. "Thank you, but in all honesty, the wine and cake would've been enough." He smiles and pours the rosé wine into the glasses. As the night develops, so does the sexual tension between us. I discovered that after his gap year, he will be going back to London; he just works in the bakery part-time for some extra money. I didn't open up too much about what has led me to live in Paris and how my relationship has broken down horrifically, but I did tell him I had just been through a messy breakup and that it why he saw me crying earlier. His response was something charming like "you won't have to worry about messy breakups anymore," or "he must've been mad to leave you." Frankly, I was too lost in his eyes to focus on what his mouth was saying. I studied his face for a good while as he spoke about his life and his family.

It was somewhere close to midnight before our conversation ran dry after the many tangents and spins which we took while desperately trying to get to know each other. The chill which bit in the air had developed into frost and suddenly the banket around me did not suffice and I longed for something else to keep me warm. We are the only couple left in the courtyard; as we both giggled away, I didn't notice the other couples escape this wonderous view. I fall back onto the picnic blanket below and look up to the sky above me allowing its massiveness to consume me. My glorious view of the stars vanishes along with the calming feeling that they gave me when Matthew's face appears over me.

Kneeling by my side, Matthew holds his mouth at a kissing distance from mine—every ounce of my body awakened by his breath on my lips. He doesn't kiss me, yet allows his cold fingers to skate down my body while his mouth remains close to mine. His hand reaches my belly button which can be felt through my knitted dress and he leans in to kiss me. As I take a breath in to absorb all that he is and all that he is giving me, his hands decide to explore further. I can feel his touch vividly through my black tights as if I was wearing nothing at all; I have never been so intimate mentally without the physical intimacy to follow. The kissing between us grows with an intensity that I have rarely experienced—If

I were an alcoholic, kissing Matthew would be my Jack Daniels and coke.

After thirty minutes of steamy intense kissing, I push Matthew away from my lips slightly, "I feel like a teenager doing this here. Should we stop before it gets too far?"

Matthew repositioned his body so that his face was directly over mine, "Should we stop and do I want to stop both have two very different answers and I only like the sound of one of them." He leant in and pushed his tongue into my mouth while gripping my waist.

Smiling through my teeth as he kissed me, I pushed him away from me again, "Come on," and I began to stand from the picnic blanket. My dress was scrunched up over my bum and he playfully squeezed it as he went to stand. The midnight walk home turns into an early hour of the morning stroll as I take him the longest route possible back to my apartment for maximum 'Matthew time.'

As we get closer to the ivy-covered building, I subtly drop in that I need to be up early tomorrow, "Nelly, I don't expect to come inside don't worry. I don't want to be just a one-night stand." He plants a kiss on my forehead and waves his hand towards the door as a goodbye.

Falling into my apartment drunk on sexual tension and arousal, my smile lifts my feet from the ground and glides me into my bedroom. Collapsing onto the bed, I waste no time trying to undress myself. I don't want to waste a second that I could imagine passionate sex between Matthew and me as I serenade myself to sleep.

Luke

Awoken at 7 am by a text on my phone, I immediately lunge for it. As my eyes are still focussing on the light on the screen, it takes me a moment to realise the text is in fact from Joe and not Nelly like I had so desperately hoped. Nevertheless, a text from Nelly's brother is a step closer to Nelly herself and I am going to take anything that I can get.

As I swipe my phone open to read the paragraph from Joe, it becomes clear from his polite demeanour that Nelly has not shared the news of our breakup with him. Suddenly I am awash of confusion and hope for our relationship; if she has failed to share the news with her family of our downfall, there may be hope for us yet. I am transported out of my dream and back into my dull bedroom and dull reality by a second text from Joe.

Hi mate, I'll land at 2 your time. Pick me up please, Claire told me that she is working! As I am digesting this information and conjuring a plan to use Joe to help me get Nelly back, my phone vibrates as Joe grows impatient and calls me for an answer. Before he has a chance to say hello, I bark down the phone at him, "Yes, of course! I'll see you at two, send me your flight information!"

After a brisk, "Thanks, see you then," the line goes dead—just as I probably will be as soon as Joe finds out the truth.

Conflicted by what to wear. Conflicted by whether to prewarn Nelly. Conflicted by what exactly I should tell Joe. A morning full of confliction and very little clarity. I spend hours pacing up and down my sad excuse of an apartment until it's time to set off for Joe.

I order a taxi to the airport to take me to collect Joe. An ostentatious black Mercedes sounds two horns outside of my apartment building sounding the incoming of sweaty palms and my quickening pulse. In my baggy blue jeans and navy half-zip sweater, I crawl into the back of the taxi. Brushing my fringe away from my trembling lip, I recite the airport address from my phone. For the remainder of the drive, I am silent. The scenic trees and fields which paint the car window don't instil the same excitement which I felt on my first ride past this view when I arrived in Paris. The flourishing rose bushes and apple trees have wilted and diminished. The fields of colourful rape seed are bare and baron. Splatters of raindrops pull me from my icy dream, and I watch as we pull up to the airport.

Joe is already outside with his case, noticeable by his bright red jumper and matching red Converse. Waving frantically as I climb out of the car to greet him with a welcoming hug, he laughs, "Hello mate, long time no see ay."

I pull him in tighter for a hug, breathing in comfort from his familiar face, "I've missed you, Joe. Have you been well?" With the taxi driver ushering us back into the car, we continue our small talk almost the whole way to the apartment. Nelly was brought up several times by Joe, but as *Claire*—I get the impression that Nelly has been neglecting to call her brother recently.

As the driver parks the car across the road from my dark apartment building, Joe looks bewildered. He looks at me and looks back at the grey block of sadness several times before he makes the connection, "You live here? This doesn't look like the pictures Claire sent me. Is she inside…oh…wait. Oh mate, what's happened?" Before I could get a chance to compose myself, I broke down into tears. The emotion floors me and I can't seem to face looking Joe in the eye. After my momentary wobble, I wipe my nose with my jumper sleeve, pay the taxi driver and walk up the path to the entrance. Joe follows in awe behind me; I don't think this is quite the welcome he expected. Joe's surprised look only grows in concern as I unlock the door and show him the dull interior of my new home. No words are spoken for a few minutes and my apartment is consumed by silence. I flip the kettle on and stand by the kitchen counter as I watch Joe navigate himself to the tattered armchair. He lowers himself slowly while placing his case beside him. Running both hands through his hair, he exhales loudly, "Oh, Luke, what's happened? I haven't spoken to Claire in weeks. I thought she was just busy, not this."

As my head falls into my hands which rest on the countertop, I begin to shake. My shoulders jerk up and down as I try to contain how distraught I am feeling. Not wanting to lie to Joe, but also determined to hide the truth, I remain silent. The only sounds which resonate from my body are that of my tears and whimpering. My croaky voice breaks through my tears as I try to explain the situation. "She left me, Joe. But she had to. I can't even say this to you, Joe. Just know that I don't blame her for leaving me. But I'll get her back. I will do anything to get her back."

The silence resumes. I can see Joe mentally processing the information that I have just vomited at him. While I wait for a response, I imagine all the ways in which Joe is likely to hurt me. Out of all of the ways I imagine, nothing could hurt me as much as I hurt her. The longest ten minutes pass and Joe exhales deeply, lifts himself from the armchair, strides over to me and hugs me. An unexpected reaction to say the least. He pulls away from the hug and stares directly into my eyes, "I don't want to know what happened, that's none of my business. I hope that you can fix this. And if you do get back together, and you hurt her again, then it will be my business."

I nod understandingly and edge a step backwards. Joe then collects his things and waits downstairs for a taxi to Nelly's apartment. Overwhelmed and exhausted by an unexpected day, I take myself off to bed.

Just over two hours pass and I am awoken by my phone's ringtone; it's Joe. Still half asleep, I roll over and hold the phone up to my ear, "Hiya mate, it's Joe. I'm just leaving Claire's for a walk. I need to clear my head after the afternoon I've just had. I'll send you a pin of my location. Please meet me; we have so much to talk about." My top lip tremors as I agree, and my palms begin to sweat.

Greeting Joe at the park bench where he sits with his fingers intertwined on his lap, I notice the dark circles under his eyes which weren't there before, and his bubbly personality seems dampened with worry. I take the seat next to him and two minutes pass until his head turns to greet mine. The worry develops before the words find their way out of Joe's tangled and confused mind. He begins to spiral and tears flood between the sentences making them almost inaudible and the only sounds I recognise are the occasional 'Claire,' 'Nelly,' 'Pen' and 'Crazy.' After a whirlwind of emotion, Joe grounds to a halt and I inhale a deep breath and digest the word vomit which has just drenched me. His head hangs low and he doesn't meet my eyes for my response; he looks drained. After another silent few minutes, he exhales, "It's like she has gone back in time and forgotten Pen ever died. She was asking me how she was and why she wasn't returning her calls. Luke, what's happened?"

I didn't realise things had gotten so bad—my head lowered to meet his. We both sit shrouded in disdain for a while until I pick myself up and stand over Joe, "We need to think of a plan." Joe's eyes wide with tears and confusion open and close slowly as he is still processing his interaction with his sister.

Several hours morph into a whole night and we are still firmly seated on the park bench. Joe and I decide that we have to help Claire or Nelly or whoever she is. We agreed to call her Nelly and retire 'Claire' for now, in the hope that one day the name will return and so will our girl. "I have to come clean and tell you what happened between us. You are going to hate me and it's likely that you'll punch me, but we need to work together for Nelly, Joe. It was bad. We fought a hell of a lot. The perfect relationship which arrived in Paris, was barely surviving. One night after a massive argument, I took things too far and I hurt her, Joe." I had to pause between sentences to swallow the tears which spilt into my mouth. "I hurt her worse than she should have ever been hurt, ever. It was awful and I am still beating myself up about it. I know that she will probably never forgive me. But I want to help you get her back to the old Nelly for you and for herself. She deserves the world; I just wish I could've given that to her."

As I wipe my nose on my shirt sleeve, Joe bluntly retaliates, "Did you hit her or cheat on her?"

Shaking my head violently trying to shake the flashback out of my memory, I cowardly whisper at the pavement, "I did things to her when she definitely didn't want me to, Joe."

The next few minutes were a blur and as my eyes opened again, the tears cleared, and I found my cheek kissing the pavement at Joe's feet. He rightly so gave me the beating that I deserved, and I accepted my fate as the first punch landed just above my eyebrow. Laying on the ground feeling sorry for myself, a strong and blood-sprayed hand was offered out to me in my pit of desolation, "Get up." Keen to avoid another stint of confrontation, I oblige and take his hand to help me back to my seat. Placing my left hand over my bruised cheek, I shift my body to face Joe as I nod to signal my understanding. Hanging my head in shame, the strong and blood-sprayed hand greets my back with warmth as Joe offers me an ounce of conciliation.

"Luke, I don't agree with what you've done and even if Nelly forgives you, I won't. We need to get her back for her sake, and you can be on your way." Joe's sudden disapproval was brutally honest and an incredibly tough pill to swallow and regardless of the lengthy apology brewing in my head—I could not speak.

While I struggled to digest today's events, Joe called Nelly and asked to meet up tomorrow for lunch; he didn't divulge that I would join them or that he would be stopping with me tonight—we thought it would be best to ambush her before she has time to overthink the situation.

Nelly

I can't believe that Joe is in town and Pen hasn't come. Joe seemed withdrawn yesterday when we met up, so hopefully today he will be a lot more relaxed. As I am daydreaming of Joe's reaction to all of the Parisian monuments that I am going to take him to, I slip on a red-knitted jumper dress over a pair of black tights. I layer this with my tan trench coat and slide on my cleanest pair of trainers before grabbing my bag off the sofa and leaving the apartment. Skipping down the cobbled path while smiling at the ivy climbing up the passing walls, blanketing them in beauty, I twist my hair between my fingers in anticipation of what today will bring. Joe texted me the address of where to meet him for lunch; this part of the city is so beautiful and quiet and a surprising choice for Joe.

Dazed in the idyllic scenery, I fail to pay attention to which bakery I have landed at. The uncanny coincidence that Joe picked the one bakery in Paris and the baker has the hots for his sister, plants a smile across my face as I stumble through the door. As the bell chimes above my head, two piercing eyes grip my attention from across the counter. As Matthew stands, his muscular outline grows, in turn making me feel intimidatingly vulnerable. I battle his charm by throwing him a gentle wave of my fingers as I scan the cosy bakery for Joe. The butterflies in my stomach are damped when the back of a customer's head looks familiar, but not because it's Joe.

Distracting me from my own confusion, I notice Joe's bright smile and giant wave from in front of the curious stranger. Striding over to investigate, it is the smell which hits me first. The specific smell of aftershave transports me back to my life with Luke. The pungent flowery undertones coat my nose as I breathe in his scent like an addict. My eye contact flits from the back of Luke's neck where his t-shirt kisses his smooth skin and darts directly to Joe.

Smiling through the tension, Joe taps the seat next to him, signalling me to join him in the leather booth. I hold my eye contact firmly, attempting to escape the gaze of Luke's suffocating eyes. "I'm sorry that he's here, but he just wants to talk. I know what happened, Nelly." My name sounds over-rehearsed and forced as it ricochets through my ears and spills out onto the floor. My eyes narrow as my nails dig into the palms of my hands while my fists clench. Joe offers me a reassuring nudge to my shoulder and my eyes jump to Luke. Suddenly I look through Luke's chiselled jaw and wide eyes and I find myself navigating my way to catch Matthew's eye. My tapping leg and shaking hands are calmed by Matthew's intimidating glance. Clouded in lust, I fail to notice Matthew gliding over to our table. The heat in my cheeks erupts as I suddenly become flushed.

Matthew looks between Luke, Joe and me several times as if he is at a tennis match. Giggling in my head at the irony of this situation and revelling in the fact that I am the only member of this foursome who knows the full story about everyone else's connection. Matthew coughs me out of my trance and greets me with a, "Hello again, please may I take your order?"

Luke's eyes narrow; as do Joe's. "I'll have a hot chocolate with whipped cream and the boys will have a coffee with milk each." I ignore their concern. Luke and Joe suddenly join the tennis match and begin dissecting our interaction.

Nothing more than a flirtatious smirk was exchanged, yet this was enough for Luke to complete the novel. Silence consumed the table until Matthew returned with our drinks a few moments later. He dusted his apron before delivering my hot chocolate into the palms of my hands. A basic exchange heightened by the subtle stroke of his thumb on mine as our fingers dance beside each other. Somehow this did not go amiss with Luke or Joe and Luke's eyebrows were practically kissing now. "Wow, the waiters are friendly here, aren't they!"

Joe's subtly sarcastic comment was followed shortly after by a tap of his foot on mine reminding me, as he always has done, to behave. As Pen was always the favourite child, Joe and I had to acquire attention in other ways; for Joe, this was football. This meant that Pen had Mum's attention and Joe had secured Dad's, meaning that I was left as the 'runt of the litter.' Joe was definitely my favourite; he helped to bring Pen back down to Earth and helped me to bite my tongue. I didn't realise that the divide was so strong until only Joe had taken the time to visit.

"How have you been, Nelly?" That is a very generic question which my rapist just casually asked me.

"Never better. Now onto you, Joe. How're you enjoying Paris and how's the family back home?" There they go, another tennis match erupts as Luke and Joe dart between each other and me in unison. After inhaling the last mouthfuls of coffee, he laughs the question off, "I want to hear about you. Home is the same old boring place that you left. Tell me about your exciting new life." I play along with his avoidance and begin by telling him all about the new restaurants which I have found and eaten at. I very much speak directly to Joe, positioning myself a little crooked so that Luke's enticing glare never catches mine.

With every sentence, I can feel my eyes creep closer to meet his gaze. With every passing minute, the scent of his aftershave crawls deeper into my nose and embeds itself within me. My pulse begins to quicken, interrupting mine and Joe's conversation. As I nod along to Joe's rebuttal so as to not draw attention to my heightened libido, Joe pauses. Matthew takes a dominating stance at the edge of the table. He asks if we are okay, which I simply cannot even begin to answer, my lips merely form a slight grin. Flushed with embarrassment, I excuse myself to the lady's room. My hands are gripping either side of the sink while I stare devilishly into the unfamiliar reflection. I scoop up the water in my hands and splash it onto my face before returning to the mirror. There are now two faces staring back at me in the mirror.

As I take in a sharp breath of air and spin my body to face my acquaintance, I fall back into the sink. He lets out a sheepish giggle and threads his hands around my body until they are intertwined behind my back. "Are you really going to pretend like I am just your waiter and you are just my customer?" His eyebrows narrow as his words trickle down my throat. Without breaking eye contact, my body remains still yet my face travels towards him. My right hand finds refuge clutching onto the back of his neck and my lips explore his ear.

I place a soft kiss on his earlobe and whisper, "If I'm not just a customer, prove it."

Before another breath leaves my body, my bottom has been lifted and placed onto the sink with my right leg pulled tight around his back. My neck and breasts are suddenly suffocated by his lips as he navigates his way around my body. My mouth is free to moan and pant as he pulls down my tights. As if he is not wasting a second, he only pulls them halfway down my legs until he unbuttons his jeans. My head falls back to rest on the mirror behind me as my body is at mercy to Matthew. Before I can comprehend the situation, Matthew is inside of me, thrusting me against the restroom sink—in the complete open—in his bakery—while my brother and ex-fiancé are in the next room. As quickly as the heat was ignited and erupted into passionate flames, it was extinguished. I became acutely aware that my brother was sitting with the man who sparked this arousal in me and was waiting for me no less than 100 feet away. I sigh heavily as I push Matthew backwards by his shoulders. His eyes widen and his bottom lip drops open. "I'm sorry, but this isn't the right time. They are waiting for me." Before he has time to digest my rejection, I plant a kiss on his cheek, readjust my clothes and leave the bathroom.

Returning to the table, I take my seat and stroke my hair flat as I greet Joe and Luke again. As I listen in on their harmless conversation about dinner plans, I keep an eye on the lady's room door, which Matthew doesn't exit for at least ten minutes after me. I cannot help but wonder what was going through Matthew's head in those ten minutes which he had alone. Scanning my audience, I notice two pairs of narrowed eyebrows. Joe looks at me with disapproval and Luke glares through me as if he is not willing to accept what he knows I have just done. Blinking himself back to reality, Luke confronts me—"Nelly, if this is some sort of revenge act please stop. You are not being yourself and it's worrying us." Luke tips his head towards Joe to signal that it is his turn to read from the script that they have obviously prepared.

Joe wraps both of his hands over mine which were knitted together and resting on the table. As he strokes my thumb with his, he looks at me with genuine concern, "If Paris is too much, we can go home."

Jolted back in my seat with his comment, my head bounced off of the back of the booth, "Joe, I am home." Luke abruptly leaves the table and slumps his way over to the till.

Now alone, Joe turns to me, "I know he hurt you, but I didn't, and this isn't how you would normally act around me. We haven't seen each other in months." I nod my head to look half-interested as the meaningless drivel floats past me. An awkward silence engulfs us until Luke returns having paid the bill. He joins in with the mute orchestra and patiently waits until Joe and I stand to leave. I trail behind hoping to catch the eye of my sneaky fling, but after a few scans of the room, I decide to assume that he must be on his break.

Luke

As the bell chimes signalling our exit of the sultry café, I exhale hoping the intrusive thoughts of Nelly and the waiter will leave me along with my breath. The unsettled feeling in my stomach is no longer down to nerves but is a direct result of Nelly's totally random actions. As she strides through the café door, I watch as her unfamiliar hair glides past a face that I no longer recognise. She tosses me a half-smile as if the reason for my stare was my unrequited love and not genuine confusion. Joe's crackled voice breaks through the icy look that I'm sporting as he suggests a light-hearted stroll to ease some tension. My eyes roll as my feet follow his footsteps; I attempt to keep up with Joe's pace in an effort to avoid awkward eye contact with Nelly.

I can hear her skipping along behind me humming a familiar tune to herself. My fists clench as I wonder *How is she so unphased? So unbothered?* Joe notices my sudden withdrawal as I become lost in my own thoughts and he attempts to spark conversation between the three of us, "I haven't seen the Eiffel Tower yet, let's head to it." Nelly manoeuvres past me and links her arm with Joe and I fall back and trail behind them. I can hear muffled pieces of conversation between the two, yet I am not involved in any. I have never felt so present and so distant at one time. Pushing my hands into my pockets, I dig out a pair of earphones.

We were standing almost directly under the Eiffel Tower before Joe nudged me out of my musical trance. Keen to maintain the peace that I had created, I avoided eye contact with Nelly as much as possible. In fact, I didn't even notice how the wind blew her hair away from her face and unveiled her rosy cheeks; I didn't notice how her dress kissed the edge of her butt cheeks which drew me in every time she took a step; and I didn't notice how she is still wearing the same necklace which I bought her for our anniversary two years ago. "Three tickets, please," Nelly requests while pulling her purse from her handbag. The gentlemanly thing to do would be to pay, but this is the least she can do.

As we enter the heavily crowded elevator, Nelly's body is pressed against mine. The arch of her back which forms her perfect bottom is pushed into me and I can hear her short release of breath as our bodies meet. I can almost hear the hairs on the back of her neck stand to attention as my breath reaches her ear. Joe is standing a mere three feet from us in an elevator full of people, yet I feel as though we are the only two people in there. I have to bite my lip in order to maintain my composure. Unfortunately, I only half succeed—my clothes stay on, but my hands wander. I run my index finger down her spine until I can take a firm grasp of her bum. I see her squirm with enjoyment as she gasps with her hand over her mouth. Joe's eyes suddenly dart to Nelly and suddenly back to the floor as he notices it was a cry of pleasure, not concern. Joe's discomfort didn't dampen my intense arousal; he was suddenly a stranger to me, and I had no shame in fondling in front of him.

As quickly as it evolved, Nelly pulled away. The doors to the elevator opened and tourists began to flood out. Despite the crowd, Joe's concerned glare managed to seek me out. I dismissed him with a smirk and brushed away his disapproval. We spent an hour up there taking various photos and trying to name the different buildings below—everything felt almost *normal* for a minute. Joe suggested that we find somewhere for an early dinner, and to our surprise, Nelly offered up her place. I was not about to turn that offer down, so I agreed for the both of us before Joe had the chance to think of something else.

As we travelled back down the elevator and headed towards Nelly's apartment, everything seemed brighter. Suddenly I was seeing Paris in the same light as when I first arrived. The smell of freshly baked bread oozed down my nose and filled my stomach. The sunset now roared like a newly lit flame instead of reminding me of what a hopeless night of drinking I had to come. I found myself looking at the hydrangea and dandelions over the unanswered texts on my phone. For the first time in months, I wasn't hibernating, and I was suddenly alive. I felt like an addict and Nelly was my drug; every drop of her attention made me sick for more.

We didn't speak much on the walk home; even if we did, I was too delusional to comprehend the conversation, let alone remember it. Climbing up the spiral staircase, I get an awful taste of déjà vu in my mouth, which only evolves as we step into her apartment. I am taken back to that awful night. I relive everything clear as day as I take a seat on the couch. Nelly takes the seat beside me, places a tender hand on my lap and whispers into my ear, "If you're struggling to be in here right now, imagine how it feels to live here."

The colours drain from my eyes and everything falls back into its dreary and tired shades. She wanted me to come here to suffer. That realisation makes my head start to pound. I feel itchy in my own skin. "What's up with you, mate?" Joe collapsed onto the couch opposite; his body lay the full width of the couch with his feet dangling from the end. Dismissing his question, I stand up and make my way to the bathroom. I splash water over my face four times before I feel ready to face myself in the mirror above me. When I return to the living room, I take the chair in the corner to prevent any further ambushes from Nelly. As she is in the kitchen, Joe and I put on the local football game on TV. Joe watches intensely in silence, while I zone out so I can ponder over today's events.

Forty minutes pass before Nelly arrives with our burgers and fries. As she places the plate in front of me, a smile creeps back onto my face, "You remembered? No salad, extra cheese and ketchup on the side."

Nelly teases me as she giggles, "I was tempted to do it wrong to see if you'd notice, but I knew you would." As a functioning addict does, I soak up every ounce of that conversation just in case that is the last bit of Nelly I will ever get. She takes her seat on the empty couch, scoffing at the football game on TV as she sits down.

I see an opportunity and I take it—"Remember when we went to that bar a few months ago and all they had on were football games? You were so that annoyed you spent the whole evening drinking gin and tonics. I had to carry you home afterwards."

Joe and Nelly start to laugh, "Hahaha yes! I couldn't keep my head out of the toilet for the whole next day!" Joe throws me a smile and starts to tell the story of Nelly's eighteenth birthday and how going to a bar with all his friends led to Nelly's first stomach pump.

Three burgers and countless stories later, I have just started the one where we had gone to a water park with Nelly's family and Joe and I threw Nelly into the pool fully clothed. Pen spent the whole drive home in just her bra and knickers so Nelly didn't have to. As Joe's laughter fades out, Nelly's silence remains. Nelly looks at Joe and frowns. "Why didn't she come? I love that you have, Joe, but I could really use a sisterly hug right now."

Joe dances around the subject and humours Nelly with, "I could use one too, Nelly." He slaps his hand on his knees and assertively offers out beers to the both of us, "Who wants a beer? We all could do with having some fun."

Joe goes in hunt of three beers from the fridge, leaving Nelly and me alone in the living room. I watch as her eyes travel uncomfortably from the palms of her hands which were nestled in her lap to the floor as they hunt for my feet. Once found, her eyes explore my body until they reach mine. Her lips part and her shoulders relax as she stares heavily at me. Her tongue appears from her mouth and lines her lips with a layer of moisture as she prepares for conversation. Combing her hair to the left side of her shoulder with her fingers, Nelly breaks eye contact, "Have you spoken to her?"

That's when it hit me. The emotional torture that I caused Nelly caused her to forget the death of her sister so that she had some form of comfort while grieving our dying relationship. She seems so convinced of this manifestation, that she is actively seeking out her sister again, as if she were still alive. Torn between trying to stall until Joe returns and not wanting the confusion to be obvious, I take the seat beside her, take her hands in mine on her lap and kiss her on the forehead. Her eyes swell with tears and longing as she dwells on why her sister hasn't reached out. To satisfy my own curiosity, I play devil's advocate, "When was the last time that you two spoke?" Hoping to release Nelly from the clutches of this delusion, I pause and await her answer.

She looks frozen in thought as if she is struggling to comprehend my question. Just as her mouth opens, Joe returns with a tray full of chocolates, packets of crisps and three beers. Nelly blinks frantically as if attempting to waft away the doubts that I have just implanted. Joe takes his seat again and I return to mine. As if sensing the tension in the room, he flicks the TV onto the music channel. Between every beat, Nelly's smile bounced back onto her face. I text Joe from across the room, "I'm worried about her." As his phone lights up in his hands, his eyes gaze down as he reads the message. He looks back up at me, with his face matching the same concerned look as mine; he nods.

Nelly

Waking up with a cloudy head and a foggy memory of the night before, I rub the mascara from under my eyes and scan my blurry surroundings. As I sit up from the hard floor, my toes peak from under the makeshift t-shirt blanket which covers me. Confused and cold, I investigate under the men's grey XL to find myself only wearing a small red thong and matching bralette. Looking down at my naked and vulnerable body, my first thought is *at least I was wearing a matching set,* shortly followed by my second thought, *where the hell is Luke?* Dread swamped me and blew my body back horizontally. Instead of feeling as cute and sexy as I did when I pulled up my skimpy red knickers yesterday morning, I feel disgusting and whorish as if wearing those knickers is a bait and that I was obviously asking for *it*. My body goes stiff and my right hand slivers down my body and into my knickers. I slide my finger inside of myself to check for remanence of *him.* I am somehow immune to my touch; where I would once be aroused, I am numb.

Sex and intimacy seem more like a business transaction now than anything else. After a thorough examination, I conclude that I definitely had sex last night—I can feel the dried semen on my thigh. My mind immediately returns to *that* night. I can remember it vividly, which is suddenly a comforting feeling compared to my current blank state of mind.

Pulling my t-shirt blanket over my head to cover my indecent body, I hunt for the villain of last night's nightmare. The living room where I awoke is bare and dated, housing only a two-seated leather sofa and a small, brown coffee table in the corner of the room. It was well-lit as there was no lampshade covering the bright bulb which hung from the ceiling and no curtains to shield it from the morning sun. An unfamiliar smell of cinnamon distracts my attention to the hallway and then to the kitchen. I see that an old-fashioned kettle is about to whistle on the stove as a pair of broad shoulders fills the room. An unbuttoned white cotton shirt is draped over them paired with some small, tight-fitting boxers which don't leave much to the imagination. Dissecting this man's back and legs, I am yet to uncover his identity. It is certainly not Luke, nor Joe, nor Matthew.

"Bonjour Madame. Ca va?" The confusion grows as the handsome stranger begins to turn around. "Ca va?" He repeats as he brushes his brunette mop away from his eyes. His delicate freckles which dance across his cheeks plaster an awkward smile on my face.

I giggle, "Paddon, Je suis anglaise." Crossing the white and grey marbled tiles to close the distance between us, he intimidatingly places his hand on the door frame at the side of my head.

With a French accent, he teases, "Oh, silly me. How are you? Did you sleep well?" Pondering over how rude it would sound to tell the handsome god of a stranger that I don't recall anything of our evening together, I nod towards the coffee, "Any for me?"

As the over-familiar French man hands me a mug of coffee, his eyes try to flutter their way into my thoughts to divulge what I am thinking. It doesn't take his piercing green eyes long to sense my confusion. "You don't remember, do you?" His thick French accent hides the understatement of the century; I giggle and shake my head. My giggle seems to be contagious as he begins to laugh and shouts "Matthew" over his shoulder. My lips part with shock as another layer of confusion develops.

"Bonjour," he whispers in my ear after gliding over to me and placing a kiss on my forehead.

"Wow! I am relieved! I'm sorry, but I can't remember anything from last night. Please, can you fill me in?"

He grins from ear to ear and chuckles, "Let's go grab some *better* coffee and we can chat," as his hand settles in the small of my back.

After scrambling back to my makeshift bed in the living room, I pull on my screwed-up dress which teases me with the idea that it was pulled off in a hurry last night. As we head out of the apartment, I tie my hair into a ponytail and wipe away the smudged mascara, making me look somewhat more presentable. We stroll to the bakery where Matthew works in near enough silence, worried that anything I say will spark some form of déjà vu causing me to remember bits of last night. Matthew takes a seat at one of the booths in the window and I slide to sit opposite. Placing my interlocked hands on the red checked tablecloth, I anxiously await his confession. "Go on."

I can see him swallow as he hunts for the right words. Both hands travel and land on top of mine, "I can't explain what happened before we met, but when you jumped out of the taxi at my bakery, you could hardly walk. You looked beautiful but your words were slurred, and you were all over the place. My friend who you met came and picked us up and I was going to let you sleep in my bed, but you fell straight asleep in the living room, and I didn't want to wake you."

I shake his hands from mine and starch my head as I think out loud, "There must be more to this."

Returning his hands to mine, he squeezes them, "All I know is that you were in quite the state when you got to me, Nelly."

My chest pounds hard and a hive of anxiety erupts within me. My palms begin to sweat and there is suddenly an unbearable itch on my skin which I cannot scratch. I think *it* has happened again. Flustered and unable to speak, I excuse myself from the booth in order to dial the number of the only person in the world who will listen to me—Pen. With each step to the door, my feet get heavier, as if I am compelled to stay inside and not make this phone call. As I reach for my phone, the screen blurs. 2…4…6…I somehow forget the fourth number of my phone password. I somehow forget there is a step to exit the bakery. I somehow forget to put my hands out in front of me when I fall.

Finally, my thoughts stop racing and I feel calm.

As my eyes open, I cannot help but let the light in. It consumes me and thrusts me awake. For a brief moment, all I am is this light. I am a beam of piercing brightness which awaits no invitation. For a brief moment, all I know is this brightness. And just as quickly as it came, the brightness left and only reality is left in its place. Unfortunately for me, reality is a pale blue and suffocatingly empty hospital room. I quickly come to the realisation that a sudden *small* trip has landed me in this position. And I even more quickly realised that this hospital room is not aligned with flowers or 'get well soon' cards or loved ones and I am agonisingly alone.

It could've been five minutes or an hour, my concept of time was very blurred, but a nurse eventually swanned in. Our conversation was just a single moment of her twelve-hour shift, but I was consumed by every word she spoke, "You've had a fall which led to a bleed on your brain. It has been two weeks and you seem to be making great strides with your recovery. Just take it easy, I'm here if you need anything."

It has been two weeks. My skin chilled. How have I been here for two weeks? Not only that but how can I awake and have only a stranger to greet me? I am taken back to those nights at home in England when I struggled to sleep. Instead of counting sheep, my mind would wander to a film-like moment like this, where I would imagine how my family and friends would flock together to await the moment when my eyes reopened as if their lives depended on it. In my imagination, the hospital room was flooded with flowers, cards and balloons which would take me days to sieve through. Reality is a far stretch from this and as the nurse exits, my heart bleeds as I pan the deafeningly silent room.

A few minutes later, the same nurse returns with a smile plastered on her face, "Your fiancé is here." Panic overshadows my confusion and sorrow as I realise that in all the hustle and bustle of the last few months in Paris, I forgot to change my emergency contact list.

Luke

She looks frightened—but that could be the pain medication wearing off. "Nelly, it's Luke. I came as soon as the nurse called to say you had woken up. Do you need anything?"
Her head resting on her pillow, she rolls it away from me and mumbles, "No." I could see her shoulders shudder up and down as tears stained her cheeks. I offer comfort from afar and hold my distance.

We sat for hours like this; a cloud of silence grew between us. The air became heavy and warm as my eyes watched the hours tick by on the rusted old watch which Nelly bought for me years ago. Just as the hands didn't tick in sync anymore, neither did Nelly and I. Just as the brow leather strap was worn and tarnished, so was our relationship. Wiping the tear which slid down my left cheek, I was pulled from my daydream by a softly spoken nurse, "Excuse me, sir, can we have a moment?" She was accompanied by a doctor who threw me a reassuring nod.

Nelly was, or at least looked, sound asleep when I arose from the plastic-coated hospital chair in the corner of the room. The doctor met me with a firm handshake and a smile, "I have some good news for you, sir."

My confusion didn't go unnoticed as he continued, "After further tests on Nelly, I can confirm that the baby is fit and healthy despite the fall." My face remains unchanged, frozen in shock. "Mum and baby have been through quite an ordeal, but both are making a speedy recovery and you should have them home in a couple of days." I am still void of emotion. Nelly is pregnant. *My* Nelly is pregnant with *my* child. To say that I cried is an understatement; I sobbed. My knees gave way and I quivered into my hands as I screwed myself into the smallest ball possible. The sound of my cries awoke Nelly who, understandably, asked what had happened. It was at that point that the doctor made his mistake—he delivered Nelly the same information that he had just unloaded on me.

We haven't had much in common recently, but our reaction to this nuclear bomb of news was incredibly alike. A few more hours passed in what felt like a blur with several conversations with different doctors and nurses which I cannot remember. Nelly and I have barely looked each other in the eye; I guess we are both just tiptoeing around some unanswered questions. The doctor revealed to us both that Nelly is five months pregnant and due in April. Fewer than 1 in 1,000 people get pregnant while the implant is fitted. I knew Nelly was one in a million, but these odds are uncomprehensible. Nelly and I haven't spoken, but I can only assume that she has done the same math as me and realised it is likely that the dreaded night which ruined our relationship, also created our child.

Our silence was infiltrated by Joe's cheer as he entered the dreary hospital room. He congratulates Nelly and me by playfully calling us 'Mum' and 'Dad,' a name which I have been desperate to be called, yet it suddenly doesn't feel right.

Nelly fell in and out of sleep for the rest of the day and into the night while Joe and I pondered over what this meant for the three of us; will Nelly want to go home to England? Given the choice, would she keep the baby? Will she let me see the baby?

Nelly was discharged the next day and Joe and I took her back to her apartment. A bunch of roses greeted us at the door with an anonymous note which Joe commandeered and read aloud, *I wanted to visit you so bad, but knew I couldn't. Let me know when you're safe and sound.* How presumptuous that the sender didn't leave a name. Nelly half chuckled at the card until she realised her audience and fell back into the silence that she had been sporting for the last 24 hours. As she took herself off to bed at ten in the morning, I took that as my cue to leave.

Joe stayed to watch over Nelly, and I took myself off to find the first place that I could think of to offer me some form of respite. I made my bed on the third pew in from the front door and asked for a neat brandy. This was followed by three pints of lager and a vodka and coke for dessert. I knew that finding out that I would be a father would be an incredibly emotional and surreal experience, but I never once imagined that I would be sat in a dark sinkhole of a bar where my tired Converse would stick to the floor and my hand would be sticky from touching the bar. I playfully told the barman while ordering my second vodka and coke that I was going to be a dad just to tease some celebration out of him. He cheered along with the familiar faces of the local French men and offered me a free shot of whisky. Four generous French men later and I was stumbling home after five more free shots. The respite I craved turned into the drunken solitude of my lonely apartment.

It was the day before Christmas Eve when I woke up, but I had never felt less festive in my life. After a few hours of wallowing in my own pity, I decided to compose myself and do something nice for Nelly; I can't even imagine how she is feeling right now. My hangover is quickly subdued by the fresh icy air on my face as I head towards the market. I spent hours deciding on the right Christmas tree and decorations for Nelly. The hustle and bustle of the busy city instilled a small amount of festivity into me. As I was sieving through the different baubles and lights, I imagined how different Christmas would be next year when I have a child to celebrate with back home in Coventry. For a second, I forgot the last six months of my life and I was just Luke from Coventry shopping for Christmas decorations for his pregnant fiancé Claire while she waits at home cooking him a Sunday dinner.

I was rapidly jolted back into reality when a bauble slipped from my fingers and rolled into the foot of a captivating stranger. "Oh, Paddon, sir. Oh, it's Luke, isn't it? Wow, I haven't seen you in months, how are you?" Coincidently, it is Nell from the restaurant which Nelly and I visited on our first night in Paris. I respond with a smile, shielding myself from revealing the horrific déjà vu which seeing her fills me with.

"Fancy a coffee?" It seems that my blunt response didn't put Nell off as much as I hoped. Unfortunately, my curiosity overtook my shame, and I took her up on her offer. We spent the next hour talking over coffee in an outdoor bar on the market. For the first time in six months, I had an hour free from obsessing over Nelly and dare I say, I actually enjoyed myself. I played devil's advocate and playfully conjured up the persona that Nelly and I were as happy as ever and were excited about the prospect of our future baby. For the first hour in six months, I felt somewhat *normal*.

After my second cup ran dry, I took that as my sign to leave. Leaving with a smile, I finally saw the light at the end of an incredibly long tunnel and saw that I could be happy again. My smile lasted all the way back to Nelly's apartment, where my smile slivered back into a little less than a frown. Nelly was still sleeping when I arrived, and Joe helped me decorate the apartment from top to bottom with Christmas decorations. We revelled in our achievement and patiently waited for Nelly to wake up.

Nelly

It feels like all I've done for the past two days is fall in and out of sleep. Reality and dream have blurred into one and I am unsure what is real anymore. To be honest, this is a state of mind that I am thankful for as reality at the moment is not something which I want to contend with. Rubbing the sleep from my eyes, I am still in the same grey joggers and sweatshirt which I left the hospital in. My life has been so hectic these past months, that I've not even acknowledged the symptoms which hinted towards my new friend's existence. Instead, I have been so caught up in my own drama that this poor human being which was created out of such a violent act, has already had the worst start to its life. I am not even a mother yet and I am already doing a worse job than my own did. I imagine that tears should fall right now, but I fear that I have cried enough tears that there are no more left in my body; instead, my stomach aches. The ache ricochets throughout my body into every bone available.

Craving some comfort which this tear-stained pillow no longer offers, I drag myself from the bed sheets to hunt for some food. While on my quest, I find tinsel strung between the lights. I venture further to find lights guiding my path to the kitchen where a freshly dressed Christmas tree stands. The mysterious decorator has also gone the extra mile and plated up some Christmas cookies on the counter. I want to smile. All I want to do is to be able to smile. My face is void of emotion. I am void of emotion. Ironically the only piece of life left in me is what is growing inside of me and what is contributing to my misery. My depressing monologue is cut off by a timid voice which I know all too well, "What do you think?" Luke says, unsure whether to approach. I look at him with my jaded eyes, unable to respond. Walking through him as if he weren't there, I open the fridge and take out a half-empty bottle of wine. While staring at him, I take a large swig from the bottle and put it back. Frantically, he dives for the bottle and pours the rest down the sink. "What the hell are you doing? Our child growing inside of you." Numb and unphased by his comment, I head back to my bedroom.

In my blue denim jeans, red turtleneck knitted jumper and bobble hat, I exit the apartment, leaving Joe and Luke dumbfounded. After a blurry and lonely walk, I end up at Matthew's bakery. The bell chimes above my head as I enter, and Matthew's eyes greet mine. They suddenly grow wide with worry and he rushes over, pushing the pastries which he was wrapping up to his colleague. "How are you? Oh, Nelly, you look awful. Sit down." And just as I thought I had no tears left in me, my body surprises me yet again and the tears stream. His ocean eyes grew so large as if he was trying to capture my tears in them. His flour-dusted hand wrapped itself around my shoulder and offered me a moment of comfort. We stayed like this for a few minutes, yet it felt like an hour. In his absence, I was accompanied by two slices of chocolate cake until his shift finished.

"I'm sorry. I didn't know where else to come. I am all over the place." He took my hand in his and led me with him like a wandering child unsure of where to go. We walked and walked and walked in silence until I felt ready to talk. By that point, it was about seven at night. I took a deep breath in and Matthew's face and darted to mine. He squeezed my hand as if trying to juice the information out of me.

I confessed everything. I told him how Luke and I had moved here for a year; what Luke did to me—twice; how I'm pregnant and don't want the baby; how I want to go back in time and start all over again. After half an hour of word vomit, Matthew repaid me with silence. His eyes were still as wide as when he found me, yet he slouched as though the weight of the world had lifted from my shoulders to his. Still, in silence, he navigates me to the next bar along the street—one I have not yet explored. "Deux verres de merlot," he orders as pulls out a bar stool for me. After a large swig of his drink, he responds, "Wow, Nelly."

I scoff at the most understated response I think I could have imagined. We both then erupt into chronic laughter. It feels so good to laugh. I laugh until my sides ache. He offers his hand out to me, "Nelly, I am here now. No matter how alone you feel, I am here now. I can help you." Matthew half smiles and continues, "I don't know this Luke as you do, but to be able to do that to someone you supposedly love twice isn't even comprehendible. We need to think about this carefully. When are you due to go home?"

My finger slides around the rim of the wine glass and I swing my feet against the bar as I embarrassingly say with my head down, "I'm due to have a baby in April, so I guess I will have to cut my internship short and will probably go home then."

He places his thumb and finger around my chin and lifts my head back up to meet his gaze, "What if you didn't? Stay here with me. I was debating whether to stay anyway, I just needed a good enough reason and now we both have one." My jaw drops and my lips part. My expression plastered a smirk across Matthew, and he chuckled while tucking his hair behind his ear.

Worry and turmoil were still present, but a new feeling was added to my roster; I suddenly felt excited. All I need to do for Luke to leave me alone is to have this baby for him. Once I have it, I can leave him to go back to England and I can stay here with Matthew. All Luke ever wanted from me was a child anyway. I convince myself that this is what will make me happy. I can have the baby and carry on working like nothing happened and Luke will be out of my life for good.

Matthew and I spend the rest of the evening pondering over the prospect of our new life before he walks me home. Even though the streets are only lit by the lampposts, Paris has never been brighter. The wind tickles the back of my neck playfully and stars radiate me with warmth. My cheeks are the only thing which hurts, as opposed to my feelings which has been a common theme lately, by the time Matthew and I make it back to my apartment. I prewarned him that Joe and Luke were home, and he shouldn't come in, so a parting kiss on my forehead was as much as I got.

Walking up the stairs, the smile slides off my face with every step I climb. Once I reach the door, there is nothing left but the distant hope of a different life. It is dark now and the

Christmas lights almost look beautiful as they are scattered around my apartment. Joe and Luke are amongst the festive decorations and put a damper on my mood. I nod towards them as a subtle thank you for their effort and take myself to bed.

Luke

It is Christmas Day and I have just woken up mid-morning after a long day session in the bar. I spent Christmas Eve alone, hoping to give Joe and Nelly some time together and hopefully spark some nostalgia that will bring Claire back to me. Panning my bare apartment, it feels more like a sad evening in November than Christmas Day in Paris. Being alone is one thing but being alone on Christmas Day is a whole different ball game. Joe did invite me over, but I thought it would be best to keep my distance—I have already ruined so much for Nelly and I'd hate to spoil such a special day too. After brushing my teeth, I find myself in the kitchen hunting for any leftover beer bottles that are lying about. After tracking one down, I make my way to the armchair when I pass the front door. I never get any post, but it looks like someone has posted me a card. It isn't stamped so I know that it was hand delivered. I take the pale blue envelope with me to the armchair. While inspecting, I notice that it has a few raindrop stains on it and it isn't until I open the card and read its contents that I realise that they are in fact tear stains.

Dear Luke,

Merry Christmas.
When we first came to Paris, I didn't expect to be spending our Christmas like this, but here we are. I have seriously gone through hell and back and I am only just seeing the end of this torment. Whether you want to accept it or not, we will not be getting back together. We can't. I will not allow myself to.

That said, I know I am carrying your child. It seems a waste of torture if you don't get what you came here for. I don't want anything to do with this child. This is your baby. After I give birth, you and the baby can leave and go back to England. I am going to stay and finish my internship. You have broken me Luke and nothing can save us.

Nelly x

As soon as I finish reading, the tears start. I slide from the armchair and sob on the floor into my hands. I am broken. It is bittersweet that I finally get to be a dad after wanting this for so long, but to not have *my Claire* beside me seems pointless. I shake my head and text Joe a picture of the card. Even though he is probably the last person who wants Nelly and me to get back together, I have no one else to offer me advice right now. Five minutes and five gallons of tears later, my phone rings. "Hi, mate, it's Joe. I don't even have any words, mate. We can go for a drink tomorrow if you want."

Struggling to get my words out, I splutter, "Yes, that would be great," and then the phone call ends and so does the only conversation that I am going to have today.

I blinked and suddenly it's New Year's Eve. Today marks the beginning of the new year and the sixth day that I have drank in my favourite dingy bar. Joe met me on Boxing Day for 'one drink' after I was seven drinks in, and I feel like I haven't sobered up since. Just as I spent Christmas alone, New Year's will also be spent in solitude. At least I will have my little girl here with me next year. We, well Nelly found out last week and then texted me, that our baby is a girl. Unfortunately, because Nelly didn't realise she was pregnant and still had the implant in for the first six months and has carried on drinking, the doctors have said that there is a high chance of some sort of learning difficulty for the baby. Nelly is so unphased and sees herself as a surrogate for my child as if she has no attachment or relation to it at all. As I swallow my third double vodka coke of the day, my rage invades me. She is purposely hurting *my* child in order to spite me. My palms start to sweat, and I can't calm down. After I finish my drink, I march down to Nelly's apartment, fuelled by rage which is only increasing with every step nearer.

When I arrive at Nelly's door, I am nothing but a walking ball of rage. I pound on the door, hoping to shake some anger with every fist which ploughs into the wood. Everything feels hot; feet to my fingertips, I can feel everything all at once. I am once again seeing red. My fists are still pounding on the door even though the door is open, and it is Nelly in front of me. I will not and I can't stop myself until I am pulled from her by Joe. Suddenly it is me who is on the ground and Joe is attacking me. Joe is hurting me when it is Nelly who is to blame for this. He didn't stop and wouldn't stop until everything was black.

Nelly

I lay on the cold floor, my body aching, tears streaming down my face, mingling with the blood that covered me. The room was silent, except for the haunting echoes of what had just transpired.

Luke, the man I once loved, lay beside me, his eyes vacant, his hands stained with *my* blood. How did it come to this? How did our love turn into this nightmare?

I tried to move, but every part of me felt broken. Luke had taken everything from me—our future, our love, and even my will to live.

As I looked up at Joe, a mix of fear and sorrow engulfed me. Luke was no longer the man I knew. He was a stranger, a monster wearing the face of the man I once loved. Joe was above me when I flickered back into darkness and woke up in another hospital room. This all-but-familiar feeling is torture. Nurses in and out, talking to Joe privately with a look of concern. I know all too well what that look is for. That is the look I give when I am on my ward and I have some devastating news to share. Joe comes in with the look of conflict across his face. I can almost see his blood boiling through his skin. That's when he gave me the news that the baby didn't survive the attack. I was numb to the news. I was paralysed by the words fleeing from Joe's mouth as if he felt wrong to even form such a sentence.

But even in this darkness, a flicker of hope remained. Hope that somehow, I will find the strength to survive. To pick up the broken pieces of my life and start anew.

With every ounce of strength left in me, I looked up to the ceiling and lay my head back on the pillow and I whispered the words I never thought I would say.

"I forgive you, Luke."

And with that, I closed my eyes, letting the darkness take me. But in that darkness, I found a glimmer of light—a new beginning, a chance to heal, and a hope for a better tomorrow.